CW01021379

SAILING MRS. CLARKSON

A SAPPHIC LESBIAN AGE GAP ROMANCE

AVEN BLAIR

Copyright Page

© 2024 Aven Blair. All rights reserved.
No part of this book may be reproduced, distributed, or transmitted in any form or by any means, including photocopying, recording, or other electronic or mechanical methods, without the prior written permission of the publisher, except in the case of brief quotations embodied in critical reviews and certain other noncommercial uses permitted by copyright law.

CHAPTER ONE: LIBBY

Sailing Mrs. Clarkson
Savannah Georgia
November 1947

Sitting on the screened back porch of my childhood home, I breathe in the familiar aroma of blooming camellia bushes. The house feels different without my mother singing and clanging in the kitchen.

Even after ten years since her death, the emptiness is overwhelming. I left Savannah for Jacksonville, Florida nine years ago, spending two years in college before heading to London, where the war felt more urgent than finishing my philosophy degree.

"Hey, Lib."

"Kyle!" I shout as I dash into his arms.

Hugging my brother with all the strength and love I have, I begin to tear up.

"Awww, Lib, you were always such a sap. I'm glad your time in London during the war hasn't changed that," says Kyle.

"Oh, hush!" I say playfully punching him on the arm. "Where are Dad and the others?"

"You know, Lib."

"Yeah, some things never change. Do they?"

"Nope. Dad, Jasper, and Lloyd are still workaholics. They're working on a big job over on Tybee Island."

"So, you're still the slacker, huh?"

"Yep! But, I give them forty hours a week. That's all they are getting from me."

"Good for you, Brother."

Sitting in Mama's metal glider chair, Kyle and I begin to reminisce and catch up on each other's lives. Gliding in the same rhythm that Mama once did makes me smile. Most women detest seeing or feeling any resemblance to their mothers. However, when your mother dies, you learn to embrace the similarities with fondness and humor.

"So, how's your photography job at the *Florida Times-Union*, Lib?"

"It's okay, Kyle, but after being a photojournalist in London during the war for four years, everything here seems meaningless."

"It's funny how you, the youngest of the four of us and the only girl, were the only one who actually saw the war. We missed the draft since Jasper, Lloyd, and I were married with kids. And you know that Dad felt like his time during the first war exempted us from joining. Sometimes, I feel guilty about not joining."

"Don't be, Kyle. I'm so thankful that you all didn't go. I doubt you'd have made it home alive."

"Are you okay, Lib?"

Gazing at Kyle, images from the war flash through my mind—powerful shots I took amid others' sadness and devastation. They had to be documented, and I know I captured each moment from the heart with every click of the shutter, but the images still haunt me.

"I'm okay, Kyle. I just saw enough devastation for all four of us."

"Maybe you just need some time with your family, Lib. I'm always here for you, and I love you, Sis."

"I know, Kyle, and that means the world to me. Your letters always brought a piece of home. I would close my eyes, and smell every single one trying to catch a scent of home. Occasionally, I imagined I could smell the sea air of Savannah. Whether real or not, your letters kept me sane, Kyle."

"Get over here, Lib."

"Oh, I'm too big for this, Kyle," I say as I sit in my older brother's lap.

"Hell no, you ain't," he says as he hugs me tight. I want to cry, and I don't know why. But I clench my left fist as I learned to do during the war to keep myself grounded, and in the moment.

Moving back to the metal glider, Kyle asked me, "Are you going to visit Jaclyn this time, Lib?"

Gazing out over the expansive backyard to the water, I say, "Yes, Kyle. I am going to see her. What do you think?"

Kyle smiles. "I think it's a good idea, Libby. I'm sure you know she's moved, and we practically rebuilt the coastal home on Wilmington Island she bought last January. It's gorgeous."

"I know; my letters were forwarded, and she wrote to me a couple of times with the new address. I always picture her in the house she had with her husband before he left—where she taught me piano lessons."

"Well, that dumbass shouldn't have left a gorgeous woman like Jaclyn in the first place. She inherited some money a few years back and invested it in stocks. Then, during the boom after the war, she sold most of it, making her very wealthy. I bet old George wishes he'd made a better choice."

"Wow, good for her. So the home is a coastal home, huh?"

"I saw your brain working when you said 'huh,' Lib. What are you thinking?"

I throw a magazine at him and say, "You know me too well, damn you."

"Well, hell, you don't share the same room with your kid sister for seven years, remain her best friend all these years, and not know her."

Laughing, I say, "That's true. You know what I'm going to do."

"Yep, you'll sail your boat right up to her dock, won't you?"

I stand and look out toward the water at my sailboat, *Paper-Moon*, my home during my senior year of high school and my time in Jacksonville. I say, "I sure am, Kyle."

Turning toward him, I ask, "Is she seeing anyone from what you know?"

"Lib, I don't see her, but the rumors around Savannah are that Jaclyn Clarkson became wealthy, moved to Wilmington Island, and became a recluse."

"A recluse?"

Kyle shrugs and says, "That's what the rumor mill in Savannah professes."

"Are you still in love with her, Lib?"

"Kyle, I don't know. We had a few correspondences through the years. What I do know is that I've missed her and can't seem to get over her. I had a few short-lived romances in London, but nothing over the last two years."

"Maybe there is a reason she's still single and reclusive, Lib."

"Maybe so," I whisper.

"You never told Dad or the others, did you?"

"Hell no, Lib. Dad would have flipped. Your secret is safe with me."

"I know that, Kyle. I just felt vulnerable about her for a moment. I'm sure Jaclyn and I are the only ones who knew about our affair, other than you. But, Kyle, I was eighteen, so it was my business."

"Yeah, Lib, but Jaclyn was thirty-seven. Not to mention a woman and your piano teacher. Damn, girl, when you step in it, you do it right."

"Oh, shut up," I say, as I shake my head and chuckle at him.

"How did it happen in the first place, Libby? You've never shared that with me."

Sitting back in the glider, I open up to Kyle about my relationship with Jaclyn. "Kyle, she was there, and I needed her. I believe she needed me as well."

"It happened one morning on the sailboat. Jaclyn knew I'd been skipping classes my senior year. I didn't give a damn about much of anything after Mama died. Anyway, she knocked on the hatch of the sailboat and caught me changing clothes and getting ready to sail for the day. One thing led to another. We sailed to a secluded, quiet inlet to talk—only we didn't talk."

"Wow! When you told me about your relationship with her, I was floored and jealous as hell."

"Jealous?" I ask with a grin.

"Yeah, like you don't know what I mean. Jaclyn Clarkson was a gorgeous woman, sis, and she still is. I bet the whole town of Savannah would love to know how an eighteen-year-old girl managed to steal her heart. Her husband was a dumbass."

"Yes, he was," I say as I gaze back at my sailboat, *Paper-*

Moon. I begin to revisit memories of how she felt in my arms and how she made me feel. I think of Kyle's question, "Are you still in love with her?" I whisper to myself, "Yes, I am."

CHAPTER TWO: JACLYN

Sipping my first cup of coffee for the day, I watch my beloved and rambunctious rat terrier, Poppy. I toss her a ball, and she eagerly retrieves it. "Good girl, Poppy," I say before tossing it out again.

Laughing at her energy, I continue the game with her, knowing it will tire her out and give us both a rest for mid-morning. Perhaps I shouldn't have gotten such a high-spir-ited dog, but she was abandoned. Since she and I have that in common, I figured we'd make a great match—and I was right. "Go get it, girl," I say as I toss her ball again.

The early morning sun casts a light golden glow over the water of my coastal home, which I purchased last year. The warm hue bathes the dock in a beautiful, bright light. This time of the morning is the sweetest; it greets me with serene peace as I sip my coffee and play with Poppy.

As I toss her ball a bit further, I notice a sailboat coasting close to the dock. Watching it, I see it get closer, so I continue to gaze at it. Suddenly, a woman throws her line onto one of the posts, and then jumps onto my dock.

Remaining quiet, I continue to watch her, sensing something familiar. My heart races as I observe her fluid movements while she ties off the boat. She is in her late twenties, wearing shorts and a navy sweater. Her short, blonde, wavy hair catches my attention as the breeze lifts it. Feeling a lump in my throat, I notice Poppy running toward her, but I can't bring myself to call her back because I'm too stunned to speak.

It can't be Libby after all these years, but I know it's her. I watch her kindness and playfulness with Poppy, who immediately takes to her and offers her the ball. Libby throws the ball toward the house, and our eyes meet and lock. She pauses for a moment. I watch her clench her fist and think *that's odd*.

With a nervous smile, I approach Libby, who seems to be nervous as well. Oh god, why is she here? My mind questions as my heart bleeds with memories of the past.

As she approaches, I'm struck by how beautiful and mature she has become. Libby was always a beauty, but the last nine years have added a confidence and depth to her beauty that profoundly moves me.

"Hi, Jaclyn," Libby says as she gives me one of her famous smiles from the past that has matured with grace and kindness.

"Libby," I whisper as she walks into my arms. Holding her, I inhale deeply. She still smells of the coastal breeze mixed with her unique fragrance. Though her aroma has subtly changed, it remains deeply familiar.

"I've missed you," She whispers.

Tears fill my eyes as I hold her tightly, never wanting to release her. But I force myself to pull away just enough to take her in visually. "My gosh, Libby, the years have only made you more beautiful. You're absolutely gorgeous."

Libby smiles at me and says, "Thank you, Jaclyn. I feel the

same way about you. You look exactly the same—you haven't aged one bit; you've only gotten more beautiful.

"Oh, Libby, stop," I say as I pull her close again. Her embrace feels different now—bold and self-assured. As I allow her to hold me, I find myself in the familiar arms of my once-young lover, now a strong yet gentle stranger. It's confusing to be held by this older version of Libby, but it's also deeply comforting and familiar.

We finally pull away and look at each other, unsure of what to say. Libby then asks, "Who is this little girl?"

"This is Poppy," I say as I pick her up. "Poppy, this is Libby. Can you say hello?"

We both laugh as Libby tosses the ball for Poppy again. "Would you like some coffee, Libby?"

"Yes, that would be nice, Jaclyn."

My heart skipped a beat when Libby said my name. I can't believe how good it felt, but I know I must push those feelings away; I can't revisit them.

I open the back French doors and see Libby standing in the yard. As I gaze at her, I notice the morning sunlight catching her blonde locks, which I've always loved. They're a bit longer now but just as lovely. The sunlight turns her hair a light, golden yellow.

"Will you come in, please?" I ask, realizing she needs the invitation.

Libby smiles and nods, following me into the kitchen. Poppy, as usual, is dancing around in anticipation of her treat.

As I grab another mug, I ask Libby, "Will you give her a treat? They're in the silver canister on the end of the counter." I smile as I watch Libby interact with Poppy, then laugh as Poppy jumps into Libby's arms, licking her silly.

"Poppy, don't be a nuisance. You can put her down, Libby. She will work you all day if you let her."

"I don't mind; she's adorable. It's been years since I've been able to have a dog, so I'm enjoying her."

Handing Libby her coffee, our eyes meet, and I feel that familiar love but also the heartbreak. "Let's go out to the lawn and drink our coffee, okay?"

"Sure, Jaclyn. Your home is lovely. I was surprised when I got your letter with a Wilmington address last year. I always pictured you at your old place, where you taught piano lessons. Your new home was unfamiliar, but now I have a reference," she says with a grin.

As we sit in the morning light enjoying our coffee, a quiet settles between us. I glance at Poppy, lying contentedly at Libby's feet, and shake my head, puzzled by how quickly she warmed up to her. It's unusual for her to take to someone this fast.

"It's so beautiful here, Jaclyn. And so peaceful."

"Yes, I love it here."

"Are you still teaching piano?"

"Not really. Since I moved out here, I just play for myself now."

"I don't blame you; if I lived here, I could forget the whole world."

Laughing, I respond, "That's what I've done. It wasn't intentional—it just happened. You know how much I've always enjoyed my solitude. Moving out here only widened the gap between me and the world."

"I can understand that. After leaving London following the war, I moved back on my sailboat, which was still docked at Jacksonville Beach. I became something of a recluse, sailing every day, much like I did during my senior year of high school."

We both laugh. "Oh yes, you and that sailboat. I'm surprised you graduated high school, but the town knew about your hurt, and everyone wanted to protect you." *Oh damn, why did I say that?*

"And you all did. Especially you, Jaclyn. Even Mr. Ellis, the principal, had a long talk with me halfway through my senior year. Thankfully, he brought me to my senses and encouraged me to enroll at Jacksonville College."

Laughing, I ask, "I've been very proud of you these past several years. I know you were studying philosophy, do you plan to go back to it?"

"Yes, I do—or rather I did. I felt the war needed me, so after completing two years, I grabbed my camera, and went to London for four years."

"Was it hard for you, Libby?"

"Yes, much of it was," she replies and I notice her clenching her fist again. I can't help but wonder when she picked up this habit and why. My heart aches each time I see her clench her fist, and I can't help but think that the things she experienced in London might be the cause.

I don't want to push her for details about the war, so I try to steer the conversation. "Libby, what brings you back to Savannah?"

"I'm not sure. I've been considering moving back for a while. I took two months off from the paper in Jacksonville to figure out what I want to do. I sailed home three days ago."

"I'm sure your Dad is happy to have you home."

"I suppose. But you know, Dad—work, work, work. I'm not even sure if he is aware that I'm staying in the guest house."

"Oh, Libby, you can't be serious."

"No, he's happy, but I haven't spent much time with him. They have a big job on Tybee, which is keeping my brothers and Dad very busy. I've mostly been alone at the house, and it's become quite haunting. Even after all this time, I still can't get used to the house without Mama in it."

I whisper, "I'm sorry, Libby."

"Oh, it's okay, Jaclyn. I have healed from the pain of her death; I truly have. I guess the house just triggers those old emotions. But I promise, I'm fine."

Sipping on my coffee, I watch her sweet face and know she isn't truly okay. She believes she is—that's how Libby copes, by convincing herself that her perceptions are the truth. But I know her too well; she is definitely not okay.

CHAPTER THREE: LIBBY

As Jaclyn returns to the house to get us another cup of coffee, part of me wants to run to my sailboat, cast off the line, and sail away. Coming here is more painful than I expected. I don't know what I expected from her or myself. It's been nine years—things change, people change. And watching Jaclyn be reserved with me is just painful. Clenching my fist, I remind myself to relax and focus on why I'm here.

Jaclyn's graceful walk always made me shudder—and it still does. As our eyes meet, she smiles sweetly at me. I smile back, rising to greet her, our eyes remaining locked. Taking my coffee, I whisper, "Thank you."

"You're Welcome, Libby." Oh god, hearing my name from her lips makes my heart leap with tender pain.

"Jaclyn, what are you doing these days now that you're not teaching piano?"

"Well, I read, play piano, listen to classical music, and do a bit of writing."

"What are you writing?"

"Oh, Libby, it's just silly musings."

"It could never be silly to me, Jaclyn," I say softly. I watch as her eyes return to mine, and she smiles.

"Well, actually, I've been writing poetry. So those are the four things I do daily, no matter what: listen to my music, play piano, read, and write poetry."

"Wow, that sounds like a lovely life. It suits you," I say softly.

"Thank you, Libby."

Suddenly, it feels as though a wall has tumbled down between us. I gaze at her appreciating her beauty, and my enduring love for this woman.

Jaclyn playfully kicks my foot and asks, "Are you going to live on *Paper-Moon* your whole life?" She asks with a grin.

"I might just do that. She seems to be the only woman who won't leave me." I say playfully.

"Oh, Libby," Jaclyn says with a chuckle. "I doubt that. I bet you had all the European women fawning over you with that Southern charm of yours."

I grin, look at her, and shake my head, taking a moment before speaking. When I look back at her, I see she's waiting for a response, even though her statement was in jest.

Bravely, I say, "There have only been two women I've ever truly loved, Jaclyn, and my Mama was one of them."

Gazing back at her after my remark, I see her eyes glistening. She places her fist to her mouth and turns away.

Things get quiet for a moment, then I ask, "Should I leave?"

She stares at me for what feels like an eternity before nodding. I rise to leave, and she stands beside me pulling me close. Whispering, she says, "Yes, you should go, but only if you promise to come back for dinner."

She pulls away, looking at me, waiting for my response. I smile and say, "I'd love to, Jaclyn. I would love that more than anything."

Jaclyn and Poppy walk me back to my sailboat. I hug Jaclyn before I climbing aboard. She unties the boat, just as I taught her years ago, then tosses the line onboard. Before I start the small engine, I ask, "What time?"

She walks up to the boat and asks, "What time would you like to come back, Libby?" My heart flutters with anxiety, and I clench my fist calming myself.

"I don't know. How about five?" I reply, trying to keep my voice steady.

Jaclyn gives the boat a gentle push and says, "How about three?"

Oh damn. I suddenly forgot how to crank the motor. I fidget with the tiller, trying to keep the boat straight. Jaclyn starts laughing at me. She knows she just unnerved me—she's always been good at that. So I nod no, then see her smile deflate. Grinning, I hold up two fingers, signaling two o'clock.

Jaclyn laughs, shaking her head in agreement. My maturity has given me the confidence and ability to unsettle a woman, too. I can tell she wasn't expecting that from me. I wave goodbye as I cruise away, knowing she still cares for me. Smiling into the warm morning sunlight, I bask in the joy it brings. I could use more joy in my life, and that woman always filled my heart with boundless joy.

Entering the small guest house, my heart is filled with a mix of excitement, and bittersweet pain. Seeing Jaclyn earlier was emotionally intense—painful yet revealing. By the time I left, I felt as though one wall had crumbled between us. Still, I'm uncertain how many more walls there are between us and whether we'll be able to break them down.

Shaking my head, I unpack my luggage and put my

clothes away in the small dresser. I sit on the bed, fall against the mattress, and look at the ceiling. A tear slips down my face, but I clench my fist and quickly wipe it away.

Sitting up, I start to smile, knowing at least Jaclyn wants to see me again. And, god knows, I want to see her. We need to confront our past to either find closure or discover if our love has endured these nine years apart. It's a journey I need to take, regardless of the outcome. I believe Jaclyn needs it, too. One thing I do know is that I still love this woman; that hasn't changed one bit.

Dressing for my date, I change clothes several times before finally settling on a pair of khaki shorts and a navy cardigan. Jaclyn used to say, "Blue is your color, baby."

Looking at myself in the mirror, I ask, "How different do I look from when Jaclyn last saw me?" I don't like the answer. Brushing my hair, I reflect on how my time in London has changed me.

Jaclyn asked me to come back for dinner, which gives me hope. Maybe she still sees a glimpse of the young Libby she once loved. Yet, I can't help but wonder, *does Jaclyn still love me?* I have no idea what she's feeling, but I know we must take this one step at a time.

As I navigate the narrow inlets and channels, I rely on the motor instead of the sails to take me back to Jaclyn's coastal home. It's a beautiful fall day, with the temperature around seventy degrees—perfect sailing weather. Smiling with confidence, I say to myself, "I'm going to get that woman on this sailboat again, even if I have to carry her on it." Then I laugh at myself.

Throwing my line over the same post as earlier this morning, I disembark and start tying off my lines to secure

Paper-Moon. As I work, I can't help but think about the first time Jaclyn and I made love on this sailboat. It brings a smile to my face.

Lost in my daydream, I feel a familiar hand gently brushing through my hair. Looking upward and over my shoulder, I meet Jaclyn's gaze. Her beautiful face is lit with a warm smile as she playfully twirls the ends of my hair.

I look up and say softly, "Hi."

Jaclyn smiles warmly and replies,"I'm glad you came back, Libby."

Standing close to her, I look into those lovely brown eyes I fell for a decade ago and ask, "Why wouldn't I?"

She nods and says, "I don't know, Libby. You said you would, but you seemed unsettled this morning, so I wasn't sure."

"Yes, I was a bit unsettled, I agree."

Jaclyn wraps her arms around my waist as we walk toward the house. "Why were you so unsettled, Libby?"

Shaking my head, I clench my hand noticing Jaclyn looking at it, then back into my eyes. She just noticed how I manage and release my intense emotions. Damn.

"Where's Poppy?" I ask, hoping to shift her focus.

"She's inside, waiting for you, I think."

Looking at Jaclyn, I smile. "That's sweet, Jaclyn."

"Well, it's true; your charm seems to have won her over," Jaclyn says with a laugh as she looks at me.

Smiling, I notice that she isn't as reserved with me as she was this morning. It seems she's had time to process our visit. Whatever happened, I'm glad she's more relaxed with me.

"I've made us a salad for a late lunch; I hope you haven't eaten yet?"

"No, I haven't. I actually have to remind myself to eat these days."

"Well, that's not good, Libby. Come inside and help me bring everything out. We can eat at the wrought iron table—-I love eating out here this time of year."

Smiling at her, I say, "Sure, it is a lovely day, and I actually am a bit hungry."

She releases me and laughs. "Good. Let's get some food in you. You're looking too thin for my liking." Her warm, genuine smile is easing some of the tension I've been carrying.

Jaclyn's eyes catch mine as we return through the French doors into the kitchen. They feel so familiar and kind—the eyes of my past. The same eyes that watched me endure so much pain. The eyes I fell in love with so long ago.

CHAPTER FOUR: JACLYN

"Thank you, Jaclyn, the salad was delicious."

Laughing, I say, "You must have been hungry; you inhaled the whole salad."

Libby laughs loudly, giving me a glimpse of my once young lover. Smiling, I realize she's still in there. The sadness and trauma she had to deal with in London hasn't completely stolen her.

I know the Libby I loved—the one I still love—is perhaps hiding in a safe place, wanting to come out but too scared to reach out. Knowing I helped her once, I feel she might let me help her again. It may be painful, but I must try to reach her. It would be more painful to allow Libby to remain hidden in the shadows of her trauma.

"Would you like some more wine, Libby?"

"Yes. Thank you."

As I sip on my chardonnay, I gaze at Libby as I still try to process the grown-up version of my young love. She's still so beautiful with those blonde locks of hair and green eyes. I could see myself falling for this grown-up version of her all over again.

Libby meets my gaze and says, "Jaclyn, thank you for saving me my senior year. I know it got deeper than we both expected, but I don't know if I would have made it without you."

"You would have made it, Libby, but I am glad my presence helped. Do you realize how much you helped me?"

Libby gazes at me as she sips her chardonnay. "Over the years, I've come to realize how much we both needed each other. At the time, I didn't fully grasp how deeply you were hurting."

"It wasn't surprising that George left me; I could never love him the way he deserved, so he found someone who could. Still, it was painful. The two of us had been married for twelve years."

"Did I help you, Jaclyn? I've often wondered if it was just my own grief over losing Mama."

"Oh, Libby, Yes, you did help me. You took me sailing so many times; those days were magical, They gave me a chance to escape from just being George's wife and the town's piano teacher."

Libby's smile and the way her eyes light up warm my heart. She needs to know that she saved me as well. She definitely did.

"Jaclyn, I've grieved for Mama many times over the years; a girl always needs her mother. The love and tenderness you showed me helped soften the blow. Dad and my brothers loved Mama, but it was straight back to work with them. Feeling abandoned is why I fled to *Paper-Moon*, as you know."

"Is that why you've stayed away, Libby?" I ask, though I know that's not the real reason.

Libby leans into the table and shakes her head.

"I don't know why I ask that, baby." *Oh damn, I just called her baby. That's what I always used to call her.*

I notice tears forming in her eyes and I see her left fist

clenched just as before. Oh, this pain is just awful. I want to pick her up in my arms, hold her close, and scare away her ugly demons. I sigh, knowing I can't do that like I did before.

Standing, I pour the remaining wine into our glasses, reach my hand to hers. "Walk with me, Libby," I say.

She looks into my eyes, smiles, and takes my hand, rising to meet me. "Thank you, Jaclyn," she says softly.

"For what?"

Our fingers intertwine, naturally falling into the same positions as years ago. We exchange a brief glance and giggle. We both know what just happened. Shaking my head with a smile, we walk to the dock and gaze at the peaceful water.

"Thank you for pushing me to live my life. I was so hurt and mad at you for a long time. I knew I loved you deeply, but I always felt like you didn't believe it, and that's why you ended things. It took me years to understand how hard and painful that must have been for you."

I swallow hard, trying to hold back the lingering pain, but it's useless. The tears begin to flow as I continue holding Libby's tender hand. Her hand is more mature and nurturing; it's wonderful. As I feel her grip tighten, I glance at her, meeting her tearful eyes.

Libby releases my hand and pulls me close. Her strong, mature arms wrap around my waist, holding me tight. I place my arms around her neck, allowing her to comfort me. Libby feels so strong; maybe she didn't come back for me to save her. Perhaps she came back to be with me, for me.

Libby pulls away, looks deeply into my eyes, and asks, "Have you ever regretted us over the years?"

Touching her cheek, I say, "Never, not for one minute, Libby. You were young, and maybe I should have regretted us becoming lovers, but I don't. I never will. I'll always remain unapologetic about how much I loved you, baby."

Libby grins, her whole face lighting up. "Good, I always hoped you didn't regret it. I often feared you might have."

Shaking my head, I whisper, "No, Libby." I place my arm around her waist again as we walk back to the house. Feeling Libby's arm around me I can't help but smile. I don't know where this is going, but maybe talking about the past is what we needed to let it go.

"Do you mind if I let Poppy out?" Libby asks.

"No, please. She needs to run for a while anyway, or she'll never sleep tonight. Which means I won't sleep."

While clearing the table, I watch Libby let Poppy out, and they immediately begin playing ball. Taking the dishes into the house, I smile at my girls having fun.

Leaving the French doors open, I hear Libby laughing at Poppy. Gosh, how I've missed that laugh. Walking back outside, I see they are still at it. "Come play ball with us, Jaclyn."

"Okay, let me clear these last dishes."

"I'll wash them if you play with us," Libby says.

"You got a deal!" I shout and laugh.

Libby and I spend the next hour or so completely tiring Poppy out. The last toss that Libby hurled for her, Poppy just laid down on her side and sighed. We both laugh at her. "Well, you've officially earned your lunch. Poppy will sleep through the night."

Sitting at the table, Libby walks over to me and says, "Would you like some ice water? Poppy isn't the only one who's tired."

I begin to rise, but Libby says, "I think I can manage it."

"There is some tea in the fridge if you'd rather have it."

"Unsweet, I'm sure. Are you still the only person in Savannah who doesn't drink sweet tea, Jaclyn?"

Laughing, I say, "Most likely. And make it two, because I

know how I got you to like it years ago. Don't tell me you've gone back to sweet tea."

Libby winks at me and says, "No way." Then she heads to the kitchen.

Gazing at Poppy, I realize how happy I am. While there are occasional painful stabs, they are nothing compared to the intensity I felt when Libby first moored her boat this morning. Perhaps we just need to spend more time together to become friends again.

"Thank you, Libby," I say as she pours me iced tea and then takes a seat beside me instead of across from me. I smile internally.

"You still make the best unsweet tea in Savannah, Jaclyn."

Choking on my tea, I start to cough uncontrollably. Libby quickly jumps up and gently pats my back, her hands firmly on my shoulders.

After I finally have command of my windpipes, I say, "Dammit, Libby, you still know how to make me laugh."

"That was a good one, Libby. I make the only unsweet tea in Savannah; you can bet your ass on that."

"Yes, you do," Libby says with a giggle. "I'm sorry, my timing was bad."

"It's okay. Your timing made it twice as funny."

Libby and I sit quietly for a while, sipping our tea, watching Poppy, and enjoying being together again.

CHAPTER FIVE: LIBBY

S pending time with Jaclyn again feels amazing. I've missed her so much all these years, and it's clear she's missed me, too.

"Jaclyn, may I ask you something?"

She turns towards me and gives me a sweet grin, "Of course, Libby."

Taking a deep breath, I ask, "Has there been anyone since me?"

Jaclyn looks at her tea glass, picks it up, and then gazes toward *Paper-Moon.* I sit patiently, waiting for her reply. She glances down briefly, then points at my sailboat and asks, "Do you see that beautiful sailboat out there?"

Looking at her, I say, "Yes."

"The young woman who owns that sailboat stole my heart years ago, so I haven't had one to give to another since."

Swallowing hard, I think of the few women I'd been with in London, and then I feel ashamed. Does this mean I stopped loving her because I slept with others? I put my hands to my face and cry softly.

"Libby, are you okay?" She asks. I nod in response

without removing my hands. Then I pull them away and clench my fist. The tears stop.

"Give me your hand, Libby." I offer her my right hand, but she shakes her head and says, "No, give me your left hand." I can't unclench it, so I don't offer it to her. Instead, I look away.

"Libby, give me your left hand." She says firmly.

Offering her my clenched hand, she takes it between her own, gently rubbing it, then kisses it. "What's this all about, Libby?"

I nod, unsure how to answer. "I don't know, Jaclyn. I began doing it in London."

I gently pull my clenched hand away and say, "Jaclyn, I can figure this out myself."

We both remain quiet for a moment. Then I stand up, pull my chair away from her, and sit on the armrest. Jaclyn looks into my eyes as I offer her my clenched fist. She takes it gently, as before, and begins to rub it tenderly.

"I've been back from London for two years, so obviously, I can't figure it out. Jaclyn, you still know me so well."

My hand begins to relax under her tender touch. We both remain very quiet as she gently soothes my hand, which holds all my sorrows. I start to move it, exercising my fingers. Jaclyn's touch still has a profound effect on me; I suppose it always will.

"I'm glad that you haven't regretted us, Jaclyn," I say as I move back to my chair and pull it close to her.

She touches my cheek again and whispers, "I never will, baby." My heart flips and tumbles at hearing her use that affectionate name again.

Southern women use that often, as well as other terms of endearment, interchangeably with friends and even strangers. However, I've never known Jaclyn to use that name for anyone else but me.

"Why did we happen, Jaclyn?"

She looks uncomfortable, so I reach for her hand and hold it. She looks at our hands and then gazes into my eyes. "Libby, many times I thought it was the grief we both had that brought us so close, but I know that was only part of it."

"What's the other part?" I ask her, still holding her eyes.

She maintains my gaze and says, "You answer that part for me, Libby."

I glance out at the water and then back at her, trying to think why, and then it finally hits me. She sees it on my face because she smiles sweetly at me. I whisper, "Because we fell in love, Jaclyn."

She touches my cheek and nods with tears in her eyes.

It was as simple as that. All this time, I'd tried to make it more complicated, thinking it was our grief, my feelings of abandonment, and everything else except the glaringly obvious reason. We simply fell in love.

As I lie in the guest house bedroom on the property of my home place, I can't think of anything but Jaclyn. Today with her was so wonderful and familiar. We talked about the past, laughed, and became comfortable with one another again.

Getting her to agree to go sailing with me tomorrow was a triumph. I feared she might resist, worried that being on my boat could stir painful memories. However, she was completely okay with it. She knows I'm an avid sailor, so that isn't a concern for her. Whatever prompted her to accept my offer willingly, I'll take it.

Turning on my side, I inhale and smell Jaclyn. Her lovely perfume lingers on my arms and in my hair. I decided to wait until morning to shower, wanting to sleep and dream with Jaclyn's intoxicating fragrance lingering on my body. With that, I drift off with anticipation for tomorrow.

Drying off after my shower, I hear a knock on the door. I wonder who that could be. Walking to the door with only my towel wrapped around me, I ask, "Who is it?"

"It's the Big Bad Wolf," says Kyle gruffly.

I open the door and say, "You ass. Well, come on in. There's nothing new here that you haven't seen before, except now it's twenty years older. So turn around while I put my clothes on."

Kyle sits on the bed with his head turned while I dress, "Where are you heading so early, sis?"

"Out," I say and laugh.

"Uh-huh, I know exactly where you're heading. So you've seen Jaclyn, then?"

"Yes, I have, and you were right. She's still absolutely gorgeous. Catching a glimpse of Kyle's handsomeness, I add, "You can turn around now."

Kyle is a good-looking guy with the same hair color and texture as mine. Except for the age difference, we could be twins—that's what everyone always said. I think a lot of it has to do with the amount of time we spent together as kids. He and I share a lot of the same mannerisms.

"Lib, the other day when we talked about this, it was all just 'talk.'"

"What are you saying, Kyle?"

"I'm just concerned. You were devastated when Jaclyn broke it off. Aren't you afraid she might do it again?"

Kyle and I move to the small living room of the guest house. Sitting on the sofa, I look at him and say, "I appreciate your concern, Kyle. But this time, it's different."

"And how is this time different, sis?"

"Well, for one thing, nothing has happened between us, and I'm not even sure it will."

"Oh, Libby, save that for someone else. I know damn well it will."

"You're right, Brother. I'm not going to lie about it. I want her, and I've never stopped wanting her. Ever."

"Okay, so then answer my question."

"Kyle, Jaclyn won't start anything with me now unless she knows we will last. I was angry with her for a long time when she broke it off. But do you remember where I went after that happened?"

"Well, yes. You went to Jacksonville College and then London."

"Exactly, Kyle. She didn't break up with me; she pushed me out of the nest. To grow, to live, and to experience the world, and I did. She gave me my freedom at her own expense."

"Damn, Libby," Kyle says softly.

"It hurt her terribly letting me go."

"Well, Lib. I don't know what to say except she's one hell of a woman."

"She is indeed, brother," I say, as I kiss his head and put my navy cardigan back on, catching a hint of Jaclyn's perfume from yesterday.

As I walk the backyard toward Jaclyn's house, I see the French door slightly open, and Poppy running toward me. I hold out my arms as she leaps, flies through the air, and lands perfectly in my embrace. I lift her up and let her kiss my nose. Grabbing her ball, we start a quick game of fetch. "Come on, girl. Let's check on your Mama."

Opening the French doors, I see Jaclyn standing in the kitchen, "I'm here," I call out.

"Come on in here. I'll let you help with our food."

"Oh yum. You're making us food?"

She puts her utensils down, puts one hand on her hip, and gives me a blank stare. "Um, well," I say.

"How many times have we gone sailing that I didn't make us food?" She asks.

Laughing, I say, "I think that would be zero."

"Ding, ding, ding. You win a prize, Libby Jordan."

I move closer to her and ask flirtatiously, "And what do I win?"

Jaclyn tosses wax paper on the counter in front of me and says, "You have just won the grand prize. You get to wrap up our chicken salad sandwiches."

Giggling, I say, "I think I'll take second place. Is there a prize for that?"

Jaclyn begins to laugh and shake her head at me. "No, I'm sorry. The second-place winner has to stay home with Poppy all day."

"Why can't we take Poppy?" I ask as I begin wrapping our sandwiches.

"Libby, that dog nearly drives me crazy as it is. I don't think I could handle that much energy on the sailboat. I'd be a nervous wreck."

"I'll take care of her," I say softly.

"You'll have your hands full with the tiller, the rigging, and all the other things that need tending to while sailing."

"Well, maybe next time?" I ask sweetly.

Jaclyn gazes at me while working on our food, then smiles and says, "Maybe."

"Good," I say, relenting to her decision to leave Poppy at home this time.

"Well, I think we have everything, don't you?" Jaclyn asks.

"Yes, let me kiss Poppy goodbye and give her a treat." Jaclyn laughs as she watches me give Poppy her treat.

We make it to the boat and get everything loaded. Jaclyn removes the dock lines while I help her into the boat. Our eyes meet intimately, and it feels amazing. I hope there will be more moments like this throughout the day. I can only hope.

As we leave Turner Creek and merge into Wilmington Creek, we clear the inlets and prepare to set sail. It's still early morning, and the wind speed is approximately ten knots—optimal for sailing.

CHAPTER SIX: JACLYN

s we reach the estuary of the Wilmington River, Libby locks the tiller and begins hoisting the sails. I fall back in time, watching my beauty trim the sails that will take us to the Atlantic. Smiling at her, I see her work quickly on the Main and Jib sails. With both sails up, Libby takes her place back at the helm to navigate the tiller.

The sails catch the wind, causing the sailboat to lurch slightly. I laugh loudly and gaze at Libby, who's smiling at me. The first wind of the day just christened our voyage. God, this feels incredible—out in the ocean's vastness with the sea salt air flowing through my hair, face, and memories.

Sitting closer to Libby, I say, "Thank you, baby."

Libby smiles at me, looks up at the sail, then meets my eyes with love. "You're welcome, beautiful."

Oh god, Libby just called me what she used to call me—'Beautiful.' Was it just our familiarity together on the boat, or is there something more? I close my eyes and feel the warmth of the sunshine on my face as I replay the moment, Libby smiling at me and calling me *Beautiful.*

I swallow hard, open my eyes, and see a bottlenose

dolphin just off the port side. I touch Libby's arm to get her attention. She smiles and nods in response. As we watch the dolphin, we see that he has gained a friend. They begin jumping and gliding through the water at the bow.

"Are you ready to sail?" Libby asks.

I take a deep breath, release it, and reply, "I guess so, you damn daredevil."

Libby laughs and trims the sails tighter to gain optimal speed. "I was hoping you had grown out of this," I say as we lean into the wind. "I trust you, Libby Jordan, but this part always made me nervous."

With that, I hold tight as Libby leans *Paper-Moon* almost on her side. We glide swiftly through the Atlantic waters, feeling as if we're flying. I hold on tight and start laughing.

"You know you're safe with me, Jaclyn," Libby says, giving me an intense gaze. I hold her eyes, not wanting to look away. This moment feels magical, just like the old days with her, but even better now. Libby has grown into herself. She's still the same, but so much more. As I gaze at her, I realize that I still love her.

"It's wonderful seeing you all grown up, Libby," I say, still holding her eyes.

"Jaclyn, it feels good being with you as a mature woman. I appreciated you back then, but now even more so. I understand why you had to let me go, even though I hated it," she says, looking up at the main sail and mast.

Libby only looked away from me to check the mast, a reassuring gesture. She knows everything is fine with the sails and every part of this lovely sailboat. Her glance away was thoughtful, giving me a moment to process her words.

As the wind takes us to new destinations built on memories of our past love, I can't help but feel that I am falling for Libby all over again. This time, though, I'm allowed to have her all grown up. Is this the universe giving her back to me because I set her free years ago? But I wonder, is this what she even wants? It might not be; she may have only returned to say goodbye. I close my eyes, praying that isn't the case.

With my eyes closed, I hear Libby ask, "Remember how I wanted you to run away with me to Key West?" Then she chuckles.

Nodding at her, I smile, but I don't laugh because I remember the sincerity of my young lover's promise to take me away to Key West and love me forever.

Libby notices that I didn't laugh, and she smiles at me. "You don't know how close I was to taking you up on that."

Her fist clenches again, and I reach for it, beginning to rub it. She manages the tiller with her right hand. "Thank goodness you didn't, Jaclyn."

As I continue massaging her sweet hand, I glance up, meet her eyes, and softly ask, "Why not?"

Libby looks out at the water and then back at me, saying, "Because I doubt we'd be here together now, and I love how I feel with you at this age even more than I did years ago."

Kissing her hand, I realize she does indeed want this. Of course, she does.

Libby and I had a magical sailing day and we're back in my living room sitting on my sofa. I gaze at Libby and see she has drifted off. I look at her sweet lips, remembering how they felt and tasted against mine. I remember how every part of my young lover smelled and tasted. That's something I'll never forget and why I've had no desire to taste another woman since her.

Poppy is lying in Libby's lap, sound asleep. It's almost like she never left, but I know she did, and the heartbreak I went through was unbearable. I remember how I couldn't eat for days, I had to cancel piano lessons, one after another, because I could barely keep myself alive. I wonder if I could endure that again if she left me. I shudder thinking about it.

As I gaze at her, I wonder if she is strong enough for us. She's a bit broken, I know, but so am I. Maybe we need one another again, just like before.

"Hi, beautiful," Libby whispers to me.

Smiling at her, I say, "Hi, baby."

"What time is it?" She asks.

"Around eight."

"I have to go before it gets too dark," She says in a panic.

"It's already dark, and you aren't going anywhere, Libby Jordan."

She stands up, "I have to go, Jaclyn. We can see each other tomorrow, but I can't stay here tonight."

I cross my arms and ask, "And why not?"

Libby stands at the French doors and looks out at *Paper-Moon*. "Because I'm too frightened to stay here with you at night."

Walking over to her, I encircle her waist from behind and say, "Nonsense, I have two spare bedrooms and this couch." I release her, then add, "Take your pick, because I won't let you out on that water at night."

She turns towards me, shaking her head, "You're right; that would be foolish. I just got nervous for a moment."

"Yes, I know you did; I saw your fist."

Libby looks down at her hand, then opens it gently and exercises it more freely than before. She looks at me with surprise and smiles. My heart jumps with joy at her tiny progress over the last two days.

"Look, Jaclyn, it's better."

"Yes, it is, baby. I noticed it right away."

Libby sits back on the sofa, and I sit next to her and ask, "Well, it's too early for bed, so what would you like to do?"

"Poker or Gin?" She asks

Smiling, I say, "I don't stand a chance against you at poker, so it must be Gin."

Libby laughs at me and then goes to let Poppy outside.

"Grab the cards. Poppy and I will be back in a bit, okay?"

"Okay, but I hope you know you're going to lose."

"We'll see about that," she says as she heads out back with Poppy.

Walking to the French doors, I watch Libby and Poppy playing fetch again. I laugh at my two young ones playing, and get the cards. I hear them come back in, and I ask, "Wine or tea?"

"Tea, please," Libby says. A wise choice this late at night. After our magical day of sailing, a bottle of wine might find us in the same bedroom—a place Libby and I are too frightened to explore this soon, if at all.

As we begin playing Gin, we fall into the same rhythm, talking about our lives. Sharing funny stories from the past, Libby starts to open up to me about her time in London during the war.

"Libby, I'm sure you saw many things you can't unsee, baby. But, please know that in time, you can heal." She shakes her head at me as we continue playing.

As Libby says, "Gin," I toss my cards on the table.

"You were always a sore loser, Jaclyn. Don't tell me you still are."

"I think I just hate losing to you for some reason." Libby laughs at me and waits for me to deal. But I gaze at her and say, "I want to ask you something, Libby?"

"Okay, Jaclyn, ask me anything."

I take a deep breath and ask, "Is that invitation to sail to Key West still open?"

Libby has a shocked look on her face. She doesn't speak, so I continue dealing the cards. "You know it's November, and hurricane season is over, so this is the optimal time. Well, that's what you told me a long time ago."

Libby picks up her cards, looks at them, then lays them back down and says, "Yes, that invitation never had an expiration date. You should know that. I'll take you tomorrow, or anytime you want to go with me, beautiful."

I'm loving this confident, mature Libby. Just listen to the way she talks to me—she really knows how to speak to a woman. Where did she learn this?

I burn with jealousy for a brief moment, imagining her with those British women. But I have to stop myself—I'm the one who let her go nine years ago, and this is the woman who flew back to me. And what a mature, exceptional woman she is. She was absolutely worth the wait.

CHAPTER SEVEN: LIBBY

Sitting at Jaclyn's kitchen table the following morning, I study nautical charts, carefully noting water depth, coastline details, and safe harbors with facilities we may need. Jaclyn sits beside me and begins sipping her coffee. I look up from the maps, captivated by her loveliness, and smile.

Jaclyn asks, "Libby are we crazy for doing this? I mean, will we be safe?"

I reach for Jaclyn's hand and reply, "If I thought you were in danger, I wouldn't even consider it. Yes, you're safe with me."

Jaclyn gives me a broad smile, nods, then continues sipping her coffee as I look over the maps.

"Are you up for a twenty-four-hour straight sail to start with?"

"Wow, Libby. What about sleep?"

"We can keep each other awake, just like the old days," I whisper sweetly to her.

Jaclyn's lovely brown eyes merge with mine, and I feel

myself falling into them again, just as I did years ago. Nothing in my life has ever felt this delicate and tender.

"I'm glad you asked if the invitation to Key West is still valid, Jaclyn. This trip is going to be incredible. I haven't been this excited about anything in years."

"I can tell, Libby. Watching you pour over these charts and plan the route fills my heart with happiness."

"You realize we have to take Poppy with us," I tell her.

"Of course, Libby. After an hour or so on the water, she'll settle down. She's such a ball of energy. I didn't realize how hyper Rat Terriers are until I rescued her, but I love that little girl. So yes, Poppy is coming."

Smiling at Jaclyn, I say, "Good, because I can't imagine leaving her here for someone else to look after."

"Oh, Libby, I already know how much you adore Poppy."

I shake my head and ask, "May I have another cup of coffee, please?"

"Yes, you may. What's our first stop?"

"St. Augustine."

"Oh goodness, Libby, no wonder you asked if I'm up for a twenty-four-hour sail."

"Yes, it will give us a head start on the voyage. We can dock at The St. Augustine Marina. It's close to downtown, so we can visit shops and eat."

"That sounds lovely. I know you're on a two-month leave from the newspaper; how long can we be gone?"

"Why do you ask?"

"Well, it might sound ridiculous, but Libby, I'm not used to roughing it. So, I was hoping to stay in a few hotels along the way. I'd rather not bathe in the Atlantic all the way to Key West, baby."

Laughing at her, I shake my head and say, "You don't think I already know that?"

Jaclyn laughs and replies, "Well, I hoped that you did, but I wanted to make sure."

When we get to St. Augustine, we can get a motel for the night. We'll both be tired, and the sailboat isn't where I want you sleeping non-stop. It's comfortable enough for me, but not…"

Jaclyn interrupts and says, "Baby, I know how comfortable—and uncomfortable *Paper-Moon* is."

As I glance back at my charts, memories of Jaclyn and me making love on the sailboat glide across my mind. I look at her and whisper, "Yes, you do know." I smile and wink at her. Jaclyn holds my gaze as she sips from her coffee cup. Our eyes lock, and she returns my wink with a sweet smile.

"Jaclyn, reaching Key West will take approximately one hundred hours of sailing time. If we sail for only eight hours a day, it will take us nine days after we leave St. Augustine."

"Are you asking if this is okay, or suggesting that it might be unrealistic?"

"Neither. I'm just letting you know this trip may take a month or so, including the week we might spend in Key West. Is that okay with you?"

Jaclyn reaches for my hand and says, "That's why I ask how long you could be gone. Libby, I can keep an eye on the sails and alert you to any dangers if you're asleep, but I'm not an avid sailor. Plus, it's not healthy for you to sail non-stop for twenty-four hours at a time."

"Yes, I agree. At first, I thought we could be there in a few days. But there's no need to rush the voyage; besides, that would take the fun away. And I'm no longer as accustomed to roughing it as you might think." Jaclyn gives me a hearty laugh.

"Thank goodness." Jaclyn says, as she pours us another cup of coffee. "After I suggested it and thought about it last night, I began to wonder what I've gotten myself into."

Laughing at her comment, I say, "We'll Sail mainly during the daytime and occasionally at night if needed, but we'll limit ourselves to a maximum of eight hours of sailing each day. Does that sound okay to you, beautiful?"

"That sounds perfect."

"When do we set sail?"

"Well, I'm not sure. Maybe in a couple of days?"

"Yes, that's very doable. We'll need provisions—mainly food and our clothing—since everything else is already on the boat."

Jaclyn is sitting across from me at the kitchen table. She sits her cup on the table and whispers, "I don't know if I'm nervous or excited, Libby."

"It's a big trip, I understand. But it's going to be amazing, Jaclyn."

She nods at me nervously, then gives me her cute, bashful grin. I smile at her, holding her gaze to make her feel safe with me.

Two days Later

It's five a.m. when a knock on my door awakens me. As I rush to the guest house door, I open it to find Dad standing outside. I say, "Well, I assume you got my note."

"Yep, what's up, Lib?"

Come in, Dad, and sit down for a minute if you have time."

"Of course, I have time, Lib. Honey, since you've been home, we haven't spent much time together, and I'm sorry.

This job over on Tybee is big, and is becoming an even bigger headache."

"Dad, it's okay. I didn't expect everyone to stop their lives simply because I sailed home for a visit."

"Well, honey, I just want you to know it will be over soon. Then you, I, and the others can finally have some time together as a family."

"Maybe Christmas?" I ask, but Dad gives me an odd look.

"Well, no, at least by Thanksgiving, honey."

"That's what I wanted to talk with you about. Dad, I won't be here for Thanksgiving, but I'll be back by Christmas."

"Well, Libby, I thought you were home for a couple of months?"

"I am. Well, I mean, I was, but…" Dad looks at me quizzically.

"I'm sailing to Key West with Jaclyn Clarkson for the next month. We're leaving this morning."

Dad looks at me strangely. "Jaclyn? Your piano teacher?"

Clenching my fist, I reply, "Yes, Dad. You know I've always been very fond of her. She helped me so much after Mama's death."

Dad removes his *Jordan Construction'* cap, runs his fingers through his hair, and then puts his cap back on. He always does this when he's thinking.

He nods and says, "Well, okay, Lib. And yes, I remember how close the two of you were." Walking toward me, he adds, "Well, give me a hug, honey, but I expect you and Jaclyn home for Christmas."

Why did Dad include her for Christmas? Dad turns, opens the door, and steps outside, his back to me. Then he turns and says, "Jaclyn is a fine woman, Libby. Whatever your relationship is with her, it's fine with me, honey. I just want you to be happy."

I rush to Dad, wrap my arms around him, hug him tightly, and say, "Thank you, Daddy." He nods and closes my door. I watch him through the door's window panes as he walks back toward the main house, leaving me speechless.

CHAPTER EIGHT: JACLYN

As I watch the early morning sun light up the waters of the Wilmington River, I feel like a kid journeying to an unknown destination, filled with wonder.

Libby and I are back in the estuary where the Wilmington River meets the Atlantic. Once again, she locks the tiller and then rises to hoist the sails. I can't help but watch her. Even though I've seen her do this probably a hundred times, it never gets old.

Libby takes her place at the helm and shouts, "Are you ready, beautiful?!"

Shouting back, I say, "Yes, baby! I am ready!" Laughing loudly, I let my face soak in the warm sun, and rest my eyes on Libby's beautiful face. She's still smiling at me. Seeing her happy makes me want to both laugh and weep.

Libby begins to trim the sails, and I feel the wind catch them. The canvas sails pop with the breeze. We both laugh; it's the first wind of our voyage. Still smiling, Libby shouts, "Hold on."

"Oh damn, Libby Jordan. Okay, go ahead."

Paper-Moon begins to lean slowly as if she's bowing as Libby heels her. Poppy jumps in my arms, and I hold her tightly and say, "Get used to it, Poppy. She's a daredevil." Libby laughs.

"Now we're sailing, Mrs. Clarkson!" Libby shouts.

"We are indeed, Miss Jordan," I reply.

As we leave the estuary and head south, I smile at Libby and ask, "How far are we from shore, baby?"

"About two miles. I'm going to keep us at this distance—far enough for safety but close enough to enjoy the coastal scenery."

Libby was so young when I first started sailing with her. She was an avid sailor back then, but now she's a pro. I feel completely safe with her.

"Wait!" I shout.

"Are you okay?" She asks.

"I forgot to do this when we left my dock," I say, pulling out a bottle of champagne.

Libby begins to laugh as she watches me pour two small glasses of champagne. Handing her one, I set the bottle down and look at her. She then asks, "What shall we toast to? Key West?"

Shaking my head, I say, 'No." Peering out at the vastness of the Atlantic, I try to think of an appropriate toast. Closing my eyes, I see the young Libby playing Chopin at my piano during one of her lessons. I wonder why that memory has resurfaced. What's that about?

Glancing at Libby, I bravely say, "Let's toast to second chances." It might be a bit deep for her, but I want her to understand my intentions. Libby holds her glass and stares at me. Holding my glass out over the boat, I ask, "Was that toast appropriate, or should I toss my glass into the Atlantic?"

As Libby's eyes meet mine, her face lights up, and she almost seems nine years younger. Her war troubles have vanished, at least temporarily, but hopefully, they will stay away for a while.

Libby smiles broadly and says, "The toast was perfect." She extends her arm, allowing our glasses to touch, and softly says, "To second chances, beautiful."

As we sip our champagne, I replay her words again and smile: *'To second chances, beautiful.'* Oh god, is this really happening, or am I dreaming?

"Thank you, Jaclyn," Libby says as she hands the champagne glass back to me.

"We'll finish this when we reach St. Augustine. I know we can't sail tipsy," I say. We both laugh and continue to giggle at each other as the gentle Atlantic winds softly blow us southward.

We are about six hours into our journey, and I still feel like I am walking on clouds as I feel the breeze and watch Libby sail. Poppy has made herself at home in Libby's lap. "Are you hungry, baby?" I ask her.

"If you are, Poppy might be, too."

Laughing, I reply, "Okay, I'll get us all a sandwich."

"Wait a minute before you stand, Jaclyn."

"Is something wrong?"

"No, the wind just seems to be shifting northwest. I've noticed it northwest for a while. I'm going to trim the sail a bit. The new wind will give us a favorable tailwind, and might help us reach St. Augustine much faster."

Libby and I enjoy the new wind shift as we eat chicken salad sandwiches. "I can tell we've picked up speed, baby."

"Isn't it wonderful? Feel that breeze, Jaclyn," Libby shouts with a big smile. Sometimes, when I glance at her, I can still see the young woman who stole my heart years ago. Just looking at her then made me smile. It still does.

"It's amazing, Libby!"

Libby and I skirt across the waters of the Atlantic, carried by the new Northwest winds and our dream from years ago. We're on that trip to Key West, the one Libby promised she'd take me and love me forever.

Looking away, a tear travels down my face. I wipe it away with the back of my hand, and when I look back, I see Libby approaching. She kneels before me, kisses my tears, then pulls back and gazes into my eyes.

"It's okay, Jaclyn. Are you feeling sad?"

Shaking my head, I shout, "Are you serious? Hell no, I'm ecstatic!" I wrap my arms around Libby and pull her close. Glancing at the locked tiller, I run my fingers through her hair. She feels so familiar; I want her with everything in me. I still love this tender woman with my whole soul. Pulling away, I stare into her eyes, and she smiles at me.

"I'm glad you're happy, Jaclyn. I am happier than I've been in years. I finally have you in my life again. I've missed you terribly."

The tears fall again, and Libby kisses them away, as I hold on to her, letting her comfort and love me. She asks, "Are you okay now?"

Nodding, I smile at her. She then rises and returns to the helm. That felt amazing. I'm loving this mature Libby. I smile, thinking, how did I get so lucky, having Libby love me again?

"Libby, look at that beautiful sunset over the shoreline," I say, pointing toward it.

"It's amazing, isn't it?" Libby says, reaching out to me. "Jaclyn, please come and sit beside me."

Knowing that Poppy is asleep in the cabin, I grin and sit beside her on the other side of the tiller. I ask, "Do you have enough room to adjust it?"

"Of course, you know that. This is where you used to sit. You know how close you can get to me."

Giving her a nervous laugh, I nod and say, "That's true. I do indeed." Then, I move closer to Libby and reach for her hand, holding it gently. "How is your hand today, baby?"

"We're riding *Paper-Moon* like we used to, out in the vastness of the Atlantic. How do you think my hand is today?"

Kissing it, I say, "Hopefully, it's just fine."

Libby nods at me, briefly glancing at my lips before looking out toward the water. I'm not letting that moment slip away.

"Libby?" I ask as she looks back at me. "Do what you wanted to do just now."

She glances at my lips, and our eyes lock. Libby leans in and whispers, "You will have to, Jaclyn; I can't." Then she pulls away and looks into my eyes again.

"Is it what you want, Libby?"

In the foreground of the first magnificent sunset of our journey to Key West, Libby whispers, "Yes, Jaclyn." I feel her willingness, and I see it on her face. Yes, she wants this. She wants me. So I touch her cheek lightly as I hear her lock the tiller.

Leaning into her, I close my eyes. Our lips touch, and I taste the sea salt on her tender lips from today's voyage into yesterday's dream. This time, I feel the winds of the Atlantic Ocean shifting, their soft breeze blowing through this magical moment from all corners of the earth. Threading my fingers through Libby's hair, I feel the deep love she holds for me. It's a brief and tender moment, made even more poignant by the sound of the sails popping as the breeze from the north gains strength.

Pulling her closer, I feel her arms encircle me. She holds me tight as she opens her lips, I feel her soft, warm tongue. The familiar lips and soft tongue I've missed and longed for are finally tasting me again.

Libby pulls me tighter with her right hand, as her left-hand travels through my hair. My god, how I've missed her touch and the feel of her hands in my hair. She's even stronger now, loving me with a mature tenderness. Our mouths become hungrier for each other as we reach back in time, seeking one another. I slow down, realizing I don't need to reach back for her—Libby is right here with me. We're on *Paper-Moon*, loving each other as we did years ago.

As I release her, I pull away slowly and notice tears in her eyes. I kiss them and whisper, "I love you, Libby."

As I touch her lips with my fingers, she kisses them and softly says, "I love you, Jaclyn; I've never stopped." I nod at her and kiss her cheek, then lay my head on her shoulder. I feel Libby's strength and gentleness as she holds me.

We remain quiet as we watch the sunset on the first magical day of our voyage. This day couldn't be more perfect.

CHAPTER NINE: LIBBY

A s the dawn breaks, Jaclyn and I see St. Augustine. "Do you see the lighthouse, baby?"

"Yes! We're here, beautiful," I say, smiling at Jaclyn as I continue navigating the St. Augustine inlet.

"Take the tiller while I lower the sails," I tell her.

With the sails lowered, I start the engine to help us navigate through Matanzas Bay. "Up ahead is St. Augustine Municipal Marina, Jaclyn. They're expecting us, and I already know our dock location."

"I'm glad you're in charge, baby. I wouldn't have a clue about all the logistics."

Laughing at her, I say, "Jaclyn, you've been aboard *Paper-Moon* a million times. You could sail her with ease."

"I did enjoy sailing here years ago, I have to admit, but I knew you weren't far away, so I was never worried."

I watch Jaclyn handle the bow and stern lines, and it makes me smile. She loves this as much as I do, and seeing my beautiful woman work the lines feels amazing. Jaclyn steps onto the dock and secures the lines. She then looks down at me and smiles. Poppy jumps out of the cabin and begins barking at her Mama, who is standing on the dock waiting for us.

"Are you ready, Poppy?" I ask as she jumps in my lap.

"Oh Libby, sailing last night was magical, baby, but I'm so tired. Are you?"

"Yes, I am; I must admit that I am indeed exhausted. Let's gather our things and find a motel that will let us check in early. We can sightsee after we get some rest."

"Do you remember our conversation about roughing it?"

Laughing, I say, "Yes, ma'am, how could I forget that?"

"Well, I phoned the Casa Monica Hotel two days ago and reserved a room. I believe it's just up ahead." Jaclyn says as she laughs.

"Thank goodness—I wouldn't want you sleeping on the boat," I say, wrapping my arm around her waist.

"I'm so glad we're doing this, Jaclyn."

"So am I, Libby. It seems unreal having you in my life again," Jaclyn says as we walk into the hotel's lobby.

Entering our room, I immediately walk over to open the old wooden French double doors. Approaching the railing, I stand and gaze out toward the bay, taking in the breathtaking view. I feel Jaclyn's arms wrap around me, pulling me close. "I'm so happy, baby," she whispers.

I hug her close and smile, knowing exactly how she feels. Turning towards her, I look into those lovely brown eyes that my teenage self fell for years ago. "Did you think I would forget you in time, Jaclyn?"

She steps away from me and grabs the railing beside us. As we look out over the bay, she says, "Libby, I wasn't sure. I just wanted you to live your life. You coming back to me was something I never expected. Perhaps that's why the universe gave you back to me. That's what I'd like to think because I'd be heartbroken if you had to leave again."

Turning towards her, I look into her eyes and smile.

"Jaclyn, I feel like I've lived a full lifetime over these past nine years. Leaving you isn't even a remote possibility. I would have never sailed up to your dock if it were."

"I believe that, Libby."

Jaclyn reaches for my hand and whispers, "Let's nap, okay?" Nodding, I walk back into the room with her and find Poppy lying in the middle of the bed. We both laugh.

"I'm going to bathe, baby," Jaclyn says.

"Yes, you go ahead, then I'll take one." Jaclyn smiles at me and heads into the bathroom. As I lay on the bed waiting for her, I drift off and begin to dream. I see Jaclyn smiling at me aboard *Paper-Moon*, as it was nine years ago. She holds me gently like she used to and whispers, "I love you, baby. You're my greatest gift, Libby."

As I wake, I remember she used to say that to me quite often back then. Glancing up, I see Jaclyn coming from the bathroom in her pajamas. I smile and laugh. She asks, "What are you smiling about, Libby?"

"You," I say with a laugh. "I had a dream that we were on *Paper-Moon*, and it was nine years ago."

"Sounds like a sweet dream. Was it, baby?"

"Yes. All my dreams about you have been sweet, Jaclyn."

Jaclyn sits beside me on the bed, and I lie back on my elbows, gazing at her. "You smell wonderful," I say.

"Go get your bath, baby. I want to snuggle with you before we nap."

"Okay, I won't be long now, especially knowing you want to cuddle."

She laughs and gives me a playful pop on the butt. Laughing as I walk to the bathroom, I look over my shoulder and say, "I've missed that."

After my warm bath, I walk back into the room and feel the November sea breeze flowing through the open French doors. Looking at Jaclyn, I see that her pretty brown eyes are closed, and Poppy is asleep at the foot of the bed. As I walk out onto the balcony, I shake my wet hair and begin drying it with my towel.

Walking back into the room, I gaze at the most beautiful woman I've ever known. Overwhelmed by my love for her, I walk to her side, lean down, and kiss her sweet lips.

Jaclyn opens her eyes and pulls me close. "That was nice, Libby. Come and lie next to me, baby. I want to hold you in my arms like I used to."

"I'd love that." As I crawl under the covers next to her, we slip back into the rhythm of our love from years ago. Jaclyn pulls me close and kisses my head. "I can't believe you're mine again, Libby."

"I've always been yours, Jaclyn. No other woman has ever had a claim on me, ever."

She smiles at me and says, "I love hearing that, but Libby. I would have understood if you had found a lovely woman your age."

"But you're glad I didn't, aren't you?" I ask with a grin.

Laughing, she says, "Yes, I won't lie to you about that, baby."

"Jaclyn, you truly haven't been with anyone else since us?" I ask as I pull away and lie on my side, looking at her. She turns towards me and whispers, "No, baby."

"Libby, you are the great love of my life. There could have never been another woman."

I sit up and look at her, then glance down at my hand and see that it's clenching a bit.

"Why is your hand clenched, baby?"

"Because I have some things to tell you that I don't want to."

Jaclyn reaches for my hand and holds it gently, as she's done for the past several days. "Libby, I want to know every-thing that's happened over the past nine years. You're a grown woman now, but you're still my girl. I want to care for you and help you heal."

My hand begins to relax under her tender touch, and I look at her and say, "Jaclyn, you already know that I've been with other women, don't you?"

"Of course I do. I hope that you have," she says. She sits up a bit and continues, "Part of me has burned with jealousy knowing other women have most likely touched you—I won't lie. But, that's all part of you growing up, Libby."

"I won't say I didn't care for them, Jaclyn. I did care for them, but you're the only woman I've ever been in love with." Jaclyn smiles and winks at me.

"Why are you bringing this up?" she asks.

Taking a deep breath, I say, "Because I must tell you this before we make love again. I don't want you thinking about that when we are intimate. That would break my heart."

She touches my cheek. "Thank you for telling me this, baby. I probably would have thought about it. It's very kind of you to be so aware of that. I don't know what to say. Damn, baby, you have grown up on me."

Snuggling beside her, I whisper, "Yes, I have, Jaclyn, but you're right about one thing."

"And what's that, baby?"

"I'll always be your girl."

Jaclyn pulls me close and whispers, "Yes, you will be, Libby Jordan. And I'll always love and protect you."

"I love the sound of that, Mrs. Clarkson," I say as I smile. We continue lying in bed, cuddling and listening to the sounds of the street below.

"Libby?"

"Yes, beautiful?"

"I want us to take our time on this trip. I don't want anything on our journey to be rushed. I'm enjoying getting to know this grown-up version of you."

Inching upward, I say, "Come here, Jaclyn."

She rises, grins at me, and then lays in my arms. "Wow, Libby, this is nice. You held me in your arms many times years ago, but your maturity certainly is comforting.

Inhaling her fragrance, I find myself drifting off, holding the woman I returned to Savannah to reclaim—the one who saved me years ago when no one else bothered. Jaclyn was my steadfast love through all my heartbreak and abandonment issues. There could never be anyone else for me but her. We fell in love when I was so young, and nine years later, I'm still deeply in love with her. How could I not be?

CHAPTER TEN: JACLYN

Libby and I woke at daybreak, had a light breakfast, and then departed from St. Augustine. Now, back on *Paper-Moon*, sailing the Atlantic, heading south. The crisp morning breeze is ferrying us calmly across the water at about 8 knots per hour.

Rising, I sit next to Libby, smile at her, and lean in to kiss her soft cheek. She whispers, "Good morning, beautiful."

"Good morning, baby," I whisper in her ear. Libby responds with a big smile and a laugh. There's no need to ask why; it's written all over her face.

"Last night was incredible with you in my arms, Jaclyn."

"Your body next to mine was very nurturing. I loved having you hold me all night, Libby. God, how you've grown and matured. It feels like I have my young Libby back in my arms, but I also have this sensual, strong, and sexy twenty-seven-year-old Libby as well."

Laughing, she says, "Sexy, huh?"

"Yes, Libby. You're incredibly sexy and sensual; my core ached for you last night. I know we're taking it slow, but baby, you have no idea what you're doing to me."

Libby looks at me, winks, and my heart flips and tumbles. "I'm glad I am having that effect on you, Jaclyn. Last night, I had to fight the urge to just take you."

"It would have been amazing, Libby. However, I am glad we're waiting a while. I want to get to know this grown-up, Libby. She's still a bit of a mystery to me."

"I don't mean to be, Jaclyn. The things that happened during my time in London changed me, but my heart still beats the same…It still beats for you."

Reaching for Libby's hand, our fingers interlaced, finding their old familiar place. "Yes, you are still so familiar to me, love, I admit that. Do I seem different, Libby?"

"The day I pulled up to your dock, you were very reserved with me. I wanted to run back to *Paper-Moon* and sail away."

"What stopped you?"

"You came back outside from the house, carrying a cup of coffee. As you walked toward me, I felt as though my heart might explode. There was something about the way you looked at me as you approached—maybe I was just struck by your beauty, as I always have been."

"Oh, Libby, you're such a charmer."

"It's true, Jaclyn." She says then smiles at me.

Pulling Libby close, I inhale her scent, mingled with the misty sea salt from the ocean. "I can't smell the ocean without thinking of you, Libby. I have only visited the seaside a handful of times since you left. It's been too painful to go there."

Libby snuggles against my neck and kisses it passionately. I feel my feminine core stir for her. I begin to wonder how she tastes now. Will she still taste the same? This is all so familiar, yet so new.

She pulls away slowly and looks into my eyes, seeing my desire for her. Touching my lips with her fingers, she looks at them before cupping my cheek and bringing me closer. Our lips touch briefly, and then I feel the cool, crisp breeze flowing across them. The breeze is cold as it moves across my lips,which ache to taste her, to know her smell and flavor once more.

"Oh, my sweet, Libby, how I've missed you."

"I've missed everything about you, Jaclyn, and my heart has yearned for you."

Nodding at her, I kiss her cheek, and then return to my seat on the port side to gaze at the coastal seaside. When I look back at her, she's still watching me. She smiles sweetly and mouths, "I love you."

Feeling the tears begin to form in my eyes, I nod and wink at her.

After a moment, I ask, "Do you feel like roughing it tonight?"

She looks at me curiously. "Are you sure, Jaclyn?"

"Why not? I want to sleep with you again on *Paper-Moon*."

Libby laughs, then says, "I would love that very much."

"Where shall we anchor?" I ask her.

"The Ponce de Leon Inlet Lighthouse would be a safe spot for us. Given the current winds, I believe we'll reach it by sunset."

"That sounds lovely, baby. So we need to look out for the lighthouse, then?"

"Yes, it should have black and white horizontal stripes."

With renewed energy and the excitement of sleeping again on this lovely boat with Libby, I sit on the bench and gaze upward. At the tip of the mast, I notice a tiny flag I hadn't seen before. There seems to be a word printed on the flag, but I can't quite make it out, so I start to squint.

Finally, the breeze catches the flag, and I see it clearly. It reads, *"JACLYN."*

Tears flow down my cheeks as I look at the flag. Wiping

them away, I glance back at Libby, who is watching me. She nods, and I sit up, continuing to wipe my tears. I hear the tiller lock, and Libby approaches me, just as she did yesterday.

Looking into her eyes, I ask, "How long has that been up there?"

"Well, that one has been up for about six months. I replace it from time to time when it fades."

"Libby, my god. You must love me, baby."

"With all of me, Jaclyn. You are the love of my life, woman. Don't you know that?"

Grabbing her, I kiss her passionately, opening my mouth and soul for her. Libby meets my intensity, and our passion ignites fiercely. I feel her tongue against mine as her arms embrace me with such passionate strength. My core burns with desire. I know I should pull away, but I can't.

Libby looks back at the tiller and then scans the water. We both know the boat is secure and the breeze is constant. Libby unbuttons my linen pants. I don't protest. She eases them off of me, leaving my panties on.

Ever since Libby held me all night in her arms, I have been erotically curious about how it would feel when she takes me. Libby whispers, "Is this okay, Jaclyn?"

Holding onto her, I whisper, "Yes, Libby."

She removes my panties and places a towel on the seat to make it comfortable. Moving her body between my legs, she gazes into my eyes. "I've missed your lovely green eyes, Libby."

Libby's hand moves to my feminine mound, and I open my legs for her. Her gorgeous green eyes remain fixed on me as she finds my overabundant liquid, which has been collecting for her all night and morning. She whispers, "You're soaked."

I continue gazing at her, unwilling to release her piercing

eyes. I nod. She gathers my liquid, and touches my swollen clit. Instinctively, I close my eyes and shudder.

Her touch is still so gentle, just as I remember. As I move to the edge of the seat for her, she gathers more liquid and slips inside me tenderly. Gliding in slowly at the same slow pace *Paper-Moon* is carrying us.

Libby is soft and tender as she pushes into my depths. Our eyes remain locked as she begins to rock me slowly. She's watching me, and I feel myself open up to her. Libby is taking me on another voyage, one that is entirely independent of our journey to Key West.

She keeps at the same tender rhythm as the boat, in sync with the waves splashing against its side. Libby rocks me a bit harder, letting me know she has much more. I know she's holding back.

Whispering, I say, "I know you have much more strength, Libby, but I love it like this."

"I love being inside you again, Jaclyn. Yes, it's taking every ounce of willpower not to take you harder, but I want to love you tenderly for now."

As Libby continues, I feel myself tightening around her fingers. "Yes, baby," I whisper.

Libby pulls out gently and then begins moving her fingers in slow circles on my clit with her soaked fingers. I whisper, "You still remember how to love me, Libby."

Still gazing into my eyes, she watches as my orgasm begins to rise. "I could never forget how to love you, Jaclyn."

I grip her blonde locks of hair and hold them as my orgasm peaks. I feel myself letting go as I stare into the eyes of my young love. "Yes, Libby. It's always been you," I whisper. She gives me a tender smile, looks at my lips, and then back into my eyes.

As I begin to climax, she whispers, "I love you." Then I fall with eyes wide open, straight into those sea green eyes that I've loved forever.

"I'm coming, Libby." My orgasm is tender and intense. I feel in tune with this mighty ocean, as I fall lovingly into Libby's loving arms.

"Come again for me, Jaclyn," she whispers, pulling me to her as my head rests against her shoulder. Libby continues her tender, yet strong movements on my clit as I come again and again. Entering me again slowly, she pulls away, her gaze on my face. I shudder with each upward thrust. Closing my eyes, I relax and let her continue loving me on this deep blue sea aboard *Paper-Moon,* where we first made love.

I wrap my arms around Libby, pull her close, and say, "My god, Libby, that was beautiful." With her fingers still inside me as she kisses me deeply. Gently, she pulls out, grabs my whole body, and comforts me. Until Libby returned, I hadn't realized how much affection and nurturing I needed, but she clearly did.

We both giggle as Libby helps me put my panties and pants back on. I put my hands to my face and run my fingers through my hair as I say, "My god, Libby Jordan, you just made me come in the middle of the wide-open sea. Only you could do this to me."

We both laugh as we hug each other. Then I ask, "Where is that Lighthouse?"

Libby laughs loudly and says, "About seven hours south."

"Okay then. Next stop, The Ponce de Leon Lighthouse." We laugh as Libby kisses my lips sweetly, then heads back to the helm and unlocks the tiller.

CHAPTER ELEVEN: LIBBY

Jaclyn and I anchored in the inlet at The Ponce de Leon Lighthouse. We're far enough in to be protected if a storm gathers. Now, we're down in the cabin eating our dinner after a full day of sailing. "The sandwiches are delicious. I think you had this all planned out when you bought these this morning."

"Libby, I won't lie to you. I did, baby. As much as I like the comfort of a hotel, I've missed sleeping on *Paper-Moon* next to you."

"It will be amazing to have you sleeping next to me on *Paper-Moon* tonight. Why do I suddenly feel like I am eighteen years old again?"

Jaclyn laughs and says, "I hope it's because you're happy."

"I am very happy, beautiful." Smiling at her, I ask, "Jaclyn?"

"Yes, Libby?"

"Was today okay? I know you wanted to take things slow."

Looking back at me, Jaclyn asks, "Did you hear me protesting?"

Laughing, I say, "Even if you had, it would have been useless. I wouldn't have stopped."

Playfully swatting me with her napkin, she says, "Libby Jordan!!"

I collapse onto the settee, roaring with laughter.

"Did you pick this bad side up in London?"

Sitting back up, I look at her and say, "You know I'm just teasing."

"You picked up this bad behavior from those British girls, didn't you? Dammit, they have ruined you." Jaclyn says as she closes the paper around her sandwich.

"No, Jaclyn." I begin to cry. Damn, why did that make me cry?

"Libby!" she shouts, kneeling beside me and pulling me close. "Baby, don't cry. I'm sorry."

Sitting up, I look at her and say, "No one has ever gotten close enough to ruin me, Jaclyn. And with all of the awful shit that I had to photograph in London and then France after D-Day, there was no time for romance. Even when there was, I had so little to offer."

"Libby, my beautiful girl, please forgive me. My jealousy got the best of me, and I took it out on you. I'm sorry for the awful things you've seen and endured. Please let me hold you."

Jaclyn pulls me into her arms and holds me close, comforting me, allowing the horrific images from the war to drip from my eyes. "I'm here, Libby. It's me, baby."

"I saw mass graves, countless dead people, crying and confused children, and hundreds of wounded soldiers. I had to witness them again and again, both through the photographs I took and as I developed them. I had to relive all the horror with every image."

Jaclyn holds me with her tender love, just as she used to. While purging some of this horror is helpful, having Jaclyn hold me during this emotional release helps me process these feelings and let them exit out of me.

"You've always been my safe place, Jaclyn."

"I always will be. You're my safe place, too, baby." She holds me tightly, then pulls away to look at me. "Libby, please, look at me."

Looking into Jaclyn's loving eyes is incredibly comforting. I want to let her comfort and love me through this, just as she did years ago.

Wiping away my tears, I say, "I'm better now. I'm not sure why I started crying after your remark."

"Libby, I want to tell you something. Do you remember how you held me in your arms all night last night?" I nod in agreement. "Well, I needed that more than I realized. This new romance with you is so different, Libby."

"I feel that too, Jaclyn. Holding you all night was amazing, and I felt you needed it. Somehow, I just knew." Smiling at her, I tuck a strand of hair behind her ear and say, "You're my woman, Jaclyn. That's something that I wouldn't have even thought to say to you years ago."

Pulling Jaclyn closer, I whisper, "You're my woman, and you belong to me."

"Oh, Libby. My god, you're such a woman now." I pull Jaclyn to me and hold her with every ounce of strength I have.

"Yes, I am a woman now, Jaclyn. Your woman."

Jaclyn runs her fingers through my hair, gripping my locks and gently pulling me away to look into my eyes. "Yes, you are, Libby. You are indeed my woman, and you always will be."

"We needed this trip, Jaclyn. Look how far we've come since I've been home. I'm falling in love with you all over again, with a deeper, more mature love. Thank you for letting me back into your heart."

"Oh, Libby," she says, sitting beside me on the settee and reaching for my hand. "You have remained in my heart, baby; I've never let you go."

Nodding, I smile and hear the rumble of thunder. We exchange a look as Poppy starts barking. "Let me check everything outside and tighten up the sails. You stay with Poppy."

"Leave the hatch open; I want to make sure you're safe."

That felt good. Hearing Jaclyn's sincere concern for my safety brings back precious memories of her nurturing me. Some might view our relationship as unhealthy, but I couldn't care less. No one understands how deeply we love each other.

Everything is secured on deck, and just in time because the rain has started. Poppy barks at me as I step back down into the cabin. "It's okay, girl. You're safe now, Poppy. You and your Mama are always safe with me."

Jaclyn looks at me and nods. "Yes, I am, Libby. I've always been safe with you."

The rain starts beating against the deck. I light the oil lamp attached to the bulkhead, casting a warm, intimate glow. Gazing at Jaclyn, I notice how breathtakingly beautiful and sensual she looks in the lamp's light. "You're stunning in this warm light, Jaclyn."

"Thank you, baby." I smile at her and wink. As the rain falls harder against the boat, I wrap my arms around Jaclyn. "This is sweet, Libby. I've always loved your tenderness toward me. God knows I've missed it all these years." She touches my cheek and says, "You're gorgeous, Libby. You've always been a beauty."

"I've missed your scent. I've missed everything, Jaclyn, but your scent is what I've missed the most. The way you smell and taste has haunted me."

"Libby, we'd better stop, or you know where this is headed."

We both laugh, and then I ask, "Poker or Gin?" Jaclyn laughs loudly.

"Let me get the cards. I'm not playing poker with a shark like you. Hell no, it's always Gin."

"Do you know how much money I won playing poker across the ocean, Jaclyn?"

"Probably more than I need to know, Libby."

"It was so easy, too. Growing up, poker was all my brothers and I played. While most of my friends were playing dress-up or other games, I was at home playing poker with those three blockheads."

Laughing, she asks," Why was it so easy to win, Libby?"

"Because people always underestimate me—that's my gift. It's always worked to my advantage. Well, you're very aware of that."

"Yes, I know that, but there's one person who never underestimated you."

"I know that, Jaclyn. You're right, I could never bluff you. You've always seen me for who I am, and never underestimated me."

We begin playing Gin at the small table in the cabin, surrounded by the soft, warm glow of the oil lamps. From time to time, I catch a quick glimpse of Jaclyn's lips, aching for them.

"Libby, have you played piano since you left?"

"I've played some. Mainly only the classical tunes, the ones you love."

"That makes me happy, baby."

Smiling at her, I say, "I'll always play those, Jaclyn. I used to play Moonlight Sonata and grieve for you. It was painful, but it brought me closer to you. The sad, tender notes flowed through my soul as my heart wept for you."

"Libby, my god," she says, pulling me close. "Baby, I'm so sorry that your tender heart hurt for me. I felt breaking it off was the right thing to do."

Hugging her back, I whisper, "You made the right decision, Jaclyn; it was an unselfish act of love. I'm sorry I said that."

"No, Libby, tell me everything. This is part of our healing, the second chance we toasted yesterday morning when we set sail."

"Yes, I suppose it is." As I continue dealing the cards, I ask, "Jaclyn, during these years, did you ever think about me sexually?"

Jaclyn looks surprised. "Well, Libby." She laughs a bit, then looks at me, somewhat embarrassed. She pushes her hair back with her fingers, clears her throat, and then softly says, "Yes, Libby, you gave me every orgasm I've had through the years. I would see your face, your breasts, your lovely body. I would remember your smell and how you taste."

"Jaclyn," I whisper. "It's been the same for me. It's always been you."

She smiles sweetly at me, winks, and then softly and seductively says, "Gin."

Tossing the cards on the table, I tackle her and say, "You had me at an unfair advantage, you sexy vixen." Jaclyn laughs as I tickle her, playfully wrestling with her. We need a new game; you always beat me at Gin."

"Well, we could play old maids," she says as she laughs and wrestles with me, eventually landing on top. Looking into her beautiful face, I see how genuinely happy she is, and my heart swells with complete love for her.

"Old maids, huh?" I say, touching her face. "I love you, Jaclyn; I've never stopped."

Jaclyn gives me a soft kiss, then pulls away and says,

"Libby, you've lived inside me for over a decade. I love you, baby; you're my greatest gift."

Smiling at her, I whisper, "Want to cuddle?"

Jaclyn whispers, "Yes, baby." Pushing her fingers through my hair, she says, "And I love that much more than beating you at Gin,"

Laughing at her, I say, "Me too, and tonight it's your turn to hold me all night."

Jaclyn kisses me softly and says, "It's definitely my turn to hold you. I would love that."

CHAPTER TWELVE: JACLYN

As I wake, I feel Libby in my arms, right where she asked to sleep last night. Smiling, I remain still, feeling her breathe as the rigging lightly pings against the mast. This sound is so peaceful and familiar, I've heard this tranquil chime so many times before in the early morning hours, after nights of loving her and sweet slumber aboard *Paper-Moon*.

Libby whispers, "Good morning, beautiful."

"Good morning, baby," I reply, hugging her close and kissing her head.

"I can't remember when I've had a more peaceful sleep, Jaclyn. These last two nights sleeping with you have been amazing. My mind feels so free and unburdened."

"That makes me so happy, baby."

Libby rises, gazes at me, and asks, "Are you happy, Jaclyn?"

Touching her face, I softly say, "The happiest I've been since before you left, baby." Libby smiles, lies back on me, and sighs. I could live in this tranquil moment with Libby for the rest of my days. Being aboard Paper-Moon with her in my arms again feels surreal.

"Are you hungry?" She asks.

"Not enough to release you from my arms."

"Oh, Jaclyn, you still know exactly what to say to make me feel like I'm the center of your world," she says with a giggle.

Hugging her tight, I say, "Perhaps we should eat a bite and get moving, though."

Libby growls, making me laugh.

"Come on, Poppy. Your mama says we gotta get up." Poppy looks at Libby and yawns. Libby points at me and says, "Blame it on her, Poppy. I am all for snuggling for another few hours."

"Oh goodness, you two sleepy heads, we'll never make it to Key West at this rate."

After a quick breakfast, we set off again, sails full of wind as we head southward. Glancing at a map, I ask, "Where should we stay tonight, baby?"

"Maybe Ft. Pierce or Port Saint Lucie, depending on the wind speed. We have a good breeze right now, about 8 to 10 knots per hour.

"That sounds great," I say as I sit next to Libby at the helm."

"I love having you back here with me," Libby says with a grin.

Kissing her cheek, I hug her tightly and inhale her scent. "I love your smell, baby."

Libby locks the tiller and turns to me, her touch gentle on my cheek. She kisses my lips softly, before snuggling against my neck and kissing it passionately. "You taste heavenly, Jaclyn."

Holding a few of Libby's strands of hair in my fingers, I let her continue kissing my neck seductively, my core burning with desire. I wanted to wait until we were in Key West before we make love, but at this pace, I don't know if we can wait much longer. "Oh, Libby," I whisper.

She pulls away and says, "I'm aching for you, Jaclyn."

Gazing into her eyes, I say, "So am I, Libby. Key West was your dream years ago, so I wanted us to wait until then. You promised you would love me forever in Key West."

"Yes, I did, beautiful. And I can wait, Jaclyn. I think it's lovely and romantic that you want to wait. And Yes, I did promise you that, and It's still true."

I kiss Libby's cheek and return to my seat on the port side. Poppy jumps in my lap and starts to bark.

"What are you barking at, Poppy? Those are dolphins. Do you want to play with them, girl?" Libby asks.

Poppy continues barking at the dolphins as they jump and glide across the water. Laughing at her and the dolphins. I glance up at the mast, noticing the flag with *"JACLYN"* on it, then look over at Libby. She winks at me, and my heart flutters. I can't help but wonder, how did I win the love of this beautiful young woman?

~

Libby and I reached the inlet at Ft. Pierce. The 10-knot wind let *Paper-Moon* glide swiftly across the water, allowing us to arrive just before sunset. We checked into a small lodge, took showers, and then had dinner.

Libby and I are back in our room after a day of sailing. As I lie across the bed, Libby asks, "Would you like to walk the beach, or are you too tired, Jaclyn?"

"Libby, I am tired, baby, but let's go for a walk. I know Poppy would enjoy it, bless her heart. Plus, I'd love to hold your hand as we walk the beach."

Smiling at me, Libby reaches for my hand; I catch it and

our eyes lock. She pulls me up from the bed and wraps her strong arms around me. I laugh and smile, "You make me feel like a teenager, Libby Jordan."

"Come on, beautiful. We don't have to stay out too late."

Poppy begins to run along the beach as Libby and I laugh at her. "I think she's happy to be off the sailboat," I say.

Libby runs after her while I stand and watch them play together. The moonlight dancing across her blonde locks warms my heart. She tosses Poppy her ball, and that silly dog races after it, heading towards the water. Libby quickly grabs Poppy, clearly not wanting her to get wet and cold.

Catching up with them, Libby reaches for my hand, and our fingers intertwine. I pull her hand to my lips and kiss it. "Your hand seems so much better, baby," I say, kissing it again. Libby nods and gives me a sweet smile.

"It feels better, Jaclyn. Perhaps I just needed you in my life again. You helped me heal years ago, and here you are once more."

"Libby, we helped each other then and now. I've been very lonely these past few years, and have missed you more than I realized until you arrived. Thank you for being brave enough to come back to me."

"I've wanted to come back to you ever since returning from London but I didn't want you to see me then. I was completely broken and a mess. I still am somewhat, but I was even more so two years ago. You deserve a strong woman, Jaclyn, so I've spent the last two years working to become the woman who is strong enough for you."

Stopping us from our walk, I say, "Libby, I'm glad you waited, not because you were broken, as you say, but because you needed the time to heal and become the strong woman you are—for yourself, not for me."

Libby shakes her head and says, "Well, I am definitely

better than I was when I returned. Plus, I also know that twenty-seven sounds better than twenty-five."

Laughing, I reply, "Well, perhaps." Touching her cheek, I softly say, "Libby, I'd have welcomed you back at any age, baby."

~

Two Days Later
Key Largo, Florida

Libby and I have spent the last two days sailing *Paper-Moon*, pushing her as fast as the Atlantic breeze would carry us, eager to reach Key West as soon as possible. We broke our commitment to a leisurely cruise, sailing for ten and twelve hours at a stretch.

Just as the sun sets, I spot the lighthouse and shout, "Look, Libby! It's the Key Largo lighthouse, baby!" Immediately, I sit next to her and wrap my arms around her. "We're almost there, baby. Look at this lovely lighthouse; it's as if it's been waiting for our arrival."

"I love seeing you this happy, Jaclyn."

"Oh, Libby, I'd be this happy with you any place on this earth."

As I steer *Paper-Moon*, Libby begins furling the sails. She then comes back and sits beside me as I navigate the boat to the marina. We dock it in an open spot and disembark. Libby pays the dockmaster for our overnight stay. We then walk to the Key Largo Anglers Club, as suggested by the dockmaster, secure a room, and fall on the bed exhausted.

"I'm too tired to move, Libby."

"Me too, beautiful."

As we lie on the bed in exhaustion, Libby looks at me and says, "This time tomorrow, we'll be in Key West, where I promised to love you forever, Jaclyn Clarkson."

Easing on top of Libby, I kiss her gently and whisper, "And you're keeping that promise; we're so close, baby." Feeling her arms around me, I reach underneath her and hug her tightly. Looking into her lovely green eyes, I whisper, "I'm still so in love with you, Libby."

Libby smiles into my eyes, touches my cheek, and says, "And I'm still in love with you, Jaclyn." Lying on top of her, I trace the outline of her lips with my fingers—those are the same sweet lips that loved me years ago and still love me now.

"You're so beautiful, Libby. You've always been a beauty," I say with a smile. "You've only grown more beautiful with age. Are you hungry, baby?"

"Yes, I am. Where should we eat?"

"Come on, I'll take you to The Caribbean Club for supper. How does that sound?"

"Sounds great. Do we have time for a quick shower?"

Looking at my watch, I say, "Yes, baby, go ahead."

"Wouldn't it be faster if you showered with me?" she says with a wink.

"I somehow doubt that would make getting ready faster. I'll admit though, I love the sound of that." Libby laughs while shutting the bathroom door.

As I lie on the bed, I fantasize about how her youthful body looks at this moment, with the water from the shower head flowing over it. I'm excited to know how her nude body will feel against mine again—how she will taste and smell. I still remember Libby's scent but I long to taste and breathe it again.

I've been very casual about how I've dressed, wearing mainly comfortable cotton and linen clothing over the past several days. Tonight, however, I've chosen a dark tan, knee-length linen dress in a classic A-line style. As I check my makeup, I walk into the bedroom and see Libby lying against the bed. Poppy is sound asleep on her legs.

Leaning against the door frame, I gaze at Libby and Poppy and realize how much joy they have brought into my life. Walking to the bed, I lean down and kiss Libby's soft lips. She opens those green eyes that I love, and she smiles sweetly at me. My heart flips and tumbles as I continue gazing at my love.

CHAPTER THIRTEEN: LIBBY

As I rise from the bed, Jaclyn's mature beauty catches me off guard. "My god, you're gorgeous," I say breathlessly. Standing, I take in her seductive makeup and stunning beauty. "You're always beautiful, Jaclyn, but tonight, you look incredible. This dress looks perfect for you."

"Awww, Libby. You really know how to make a girl feel appreciated, baby."

"My love, I can't take my eyes off you." I sit for a moment, and Jaclyn walks over. I pull her close and gaze up at her as she runs her fingers through my hair. She pulls me to her, continuing to show her love. Taking a deep breath, I inhale her intoxicating perfume and say, "You smell incredible."

"Well, thank you. Come on, baby, let's go eat," she says. Rising, I take her hand in mine and smile at her.

I quickly say, "Poppy, we won't be long. You be a good girl, and we'll bring you back a treat."

Jaclyn laughs and says, "Sometimes I think you love that silly dog more than me." Laughing, I say, "I do love her, but I love her twice as much because she's yours, Jaclyn."

"That's sweet, Libby. Come on, let's go eat."

As we enter the Caribbean Club, we can't help but notice what looks like professional studio lights and cameras pushed toward one side of the restaurant bar. We then glance toward the back and see a large table full of interesting people talking and laughing.

An older gentleman approaches us, asking for our drink order. Jaclyn replies, "Please bring us a bottle of Beaulieu Chardonnay." The waiter nods, and then Jaclyn asks, "Is that a movie crew in the back?"

"The waiter says, "Yes, they are filming portions of a movie here called *Key Largo*." He leans closer and whispers, "That's Humphrey Bogart at the end of the table, and Miss Bacall is next to him."

Jaclyn and I look at him, amazed. "Well, my goodness, isn't this interesting? We are on a trip to Key West, and we just happened upon a movie set. That's incredible."

The waiter nods and smiles, then turns and walks away. Jaclyn and I look and see them just as the waiter said. "Wow, can you believe this? I never expected to see those two on our romantic getaway. How about you?"

Jaclyn shakes her head and says, "Not in a million years. Miss Bacall is very pretty, and is probably used to being the most beautiful woman in the room. But tonight, I have some bad news for her—Libby Jordan is the most gorgeous woman in this club."

"Jaclyn," I whisper, feeling a bit embarrassed as a tear begins to form.

She touches my cheek and says, "Baby, if it weren't true, I wouldn't have said it."

As the waiter pours our wine, I gaze into Jaclyn's dark eyes and smile. This club could be filled with a hundred Bacalls, and I would still be completely captivated by Jaclyn.

"You completely take my breath away, Jaclyn Clarkson," I whisper. "Make another toast for us, beautiful."

She continues gazing at me and says, "It's the same toast, Libby. To our second chance, baby." We clink our glasses together, and hear them ding lightly. Then, we sip our wine and continue gazing at each other.

Jaclyn and I are back in our room, in bed, cuddling as we have every night since we left Savannah days ago. We lie on our sides, gazing at each other. Inching closer, I realize how tired my body and mind are. "Please hold me, Jaclyn."

Pulling me to her breast, she says, "Come closer. Let me feel you." With her fingers intertwined in my hair, she kisses my head and whispers, "Good night, my sweet Libby. I love you."

"Goodnight, beautiful. I love you, Jaclyn." I say just before drifting off in her arms.

It's midmorning, and we left Key Largo about two hours ago, which means we should reach Key West within the next three hours. I feel a sudden uneasiness as the temperature drops and the wind seems to have shifted again from the North. "Jaclyn, we need to get prepared for a storm. I think a cold front is moving in from the North."

Staring north, Jaclyn says, "It looks scary, Libby."

"We'll be okay. We just need to get our rain jackets and life preservers. I'll lower the sails and start the engine."

"Okay, baby. I'll be right back."

After I lower the sails and start the engine, I feel Jaclyn beside me, holding my jacket open for me. "Thank you, beautiful," I say, smiling into her eyes. "We're going to be fine, my love. There's an uninhabited island called Rodriguez Key to the east; I'll take us there. You go down in the cabin with Poppy. Okay?"

Jaclyn shakes her head, " No, I'm staying up here with you. I'll put Poppy down in the cabin, but my place is next to you."

Smiling at her, I nod and say, "Stubborn."

She laughs and then puts Poppy below. She starts gathering up any loose items on the deck and securing them. The cold rain and wind begin to hit us, and the ocean waves grow angry.

Jaclyn is seated next to me with her arm around me. I'd prefer her to be below, but I admit her presence is comforting.

The north wind blows harder, and the rain joins it. The angry wind begins to fight with *Paper-Moon.* She's never faced a fight like this, but I trust this boat, and I have faith in her ability to ferry us to safety. Grabbing my binoculars from beneath the seat, I try to spot Rodriguez Key. Visibility is almost non-existent, but I remember seeing it just before the rain started.

With the sails down and Jaclyn next to me, I steer *Paper-Moon* east toward where I think the key is. The rain grows fierce and the wind even stronger. I'm somewhat frightened, but I keep up a strong front, as wartime taught me to do.

Knowing Jaclyn is scared, I put my arm around her and say, "Don't worry, beautiful. Safety is just ahead. I kiss her cheek and then return to steering us east. Looking through my binoculars, I still have no reference for where that Key is.

Heading eastward, I remain diligent and stoic, determined to get Jaclyn to safety. The waves have grown and are pushing us south. I increase the speed as *Paper-Moon* and I battle Mother Nature and the Great Atlantic Ocean. Looking through the binoculars once more, I finally spot that beautiful uninhabited island just ahead. I hand the binoculars to

Jaclyn, smile, and point east. She looks and exclaims, "Libby, there it is, baby!"

"Help me, Jaclyn! You're my navigator now!" I shout.

"Jaclyn and I finally reach the Key. Sweetheart, I want to be on the south tip. Navigate us there." Nodding, she starts pointing in the direction for me to take. As I'm finally able to see without the binoculars, I spot the tip of Rodriguez Key. After rounding the tip, I continue heading east to find a safe spot to tuck us in.

The rain remains incredibly fierce, but the wind and the vicious waves are calmer in our current position. "I'm going to drop the anchor now because I don't know how shallow it is closer to shore."

"Okay, baby, I'll lock the tiller." I kiss Jaclyn on the cheek and head toward the bow to drop the anchor. As I walk back after anchoring, I notice the boom has broken free during the storm. It swings toward me, hitting my forehead and knocking me backward. As I tumble overboard, I catch a final glimpse of Jaclyn's beautiful face.

As I fall slowly into the great Atlantic Ocean, I begin to dream of Jaclyn. She's smiling at me, wearing the same linen dress she wore last night, looking just as captivating.

"Where have you been, Libby?" she asks. All I can do is smile at her, unable to speak. She takes me in her loving arms and laughs. "You're home, Libby! I've waited so long for you, baby. What took you so long to return to me?" Unable to answer her questions, I feel myself simply floating in her love. All I can do is smile at her, realizing how deeply loved I am.

She then says, "Libby, take me sailing tomorrow, baby. I've missed being on *Paper-Moon* with you. I've missed sailing, cuddling, and making love to you aboard your beautiful sailboat.

Suddenly, we are sailing rapidly across the Great Atlantic

aboard *Paper-Moon,* with the wind at our back. Jaclyn is laughing at me, her beautiful face glowing. Finally, I can speak, I simply ask, "Are you my guardian angel?"

Laughing, she says, "No, Libby. I'm your lover, but I've loved you forever. In some ways, maybe I am your guardian angel."

"I hope you are both, because you are the most beautiful woman I've ever known."

"Libby!…Libby, baby!"

Opening my eyes, I see Jaclyn beside me and *Paper-Moon* behind her. "Libby, baby, are you okay!?" She shouts frantically.

As I float next to Jaclyn, I reach for my forehead and feel a large knot where the boom hit me. I hear Poppy barking, and start to laugh. Then I put my arms around Jaclyn and hug her with all of my strength.

As we swim to the stern of the boat to access the ladder, all I can do is laugh and smile. I'm still living in this beautiful and magical dream. "What are you laughing at, Libby Jordan?"

"This. Us, baby." I say with a laugh.

Back onboard, Jaclyn and I head below to the cabin after securing the anchor and the boom that broke loose.

"Libby, come here and let me look at your head. Lay in my lap, baby." Lying in Jaclyn's lap, I keep smiling. "You have a terrible knot, Libby. I'm worried."

Lying on my back, I look up at her and say, "Jaclyn, I'm fine."

She begins to cry. "You scared me, Libby." I touch her face.

"Jaclyn? Listen to me."

Wiping her tears, she says, "Okay, baby. What happened to you?"

"I had the most beautiful dream, Jaclyn. In the dream, I

asked if you were my guardian angel because you were so bright and loving."

She wipes a tear and looks down at me but remains silent. "You laughed and said, 'No, Libby, I'm your lover.'" Jaclyn's tears start again, and I bring her to me and kiss them away. "You said, "I've loved you forever, so in some ways, maybe I am your guardian angel."

Rising, I move close to her as I hold my throbbing forehead. I whisper, "Are you both, Jaclyn? Are you my lover and my guardian angel?"

Jaclyn takes my face in her hands and kisses me sweetly. She pulls away and says, "Maybe I am, Libby." Gazing into my eyes, she continues, "Libby, you've always been my lover, even during our time apart. I've always felt protective and responsible for your well-being, so maybe I am, baby."

Shaking my head with a loving smile, I say, "Yes, you are, Jaclyn. You are both."

CHAPTER FOURTEEN: JACLYN

The storm finally passed us, and we remained safe, tucked away in the cabin. About three hours later, we sailed into Key West and moored *Paper-Moon* at a marina. After checking into our beach cottage, I immediately called a doctor to come and assess Libby's head.

As Libby rests on the sofa of our cottage, the doctor begins to examine the bump on her forehead. "Miss Jordan. I don't believe you have a concussion, so you are lucky indeed. However, that's quite a bump you have. Is it very painful?"

"Yes, somewhat," Libby says.

"Well, I'll leave you this small bottle of pain pills for the discomfort. You're fortunate it isn't worse. Why were you two out sailing today?" The doctor asks.

We laugh and explain that we left Savannah over a week ago. The doctor looks astonished, as if he doesn't encounter many women who would sail that far. I smile, thinking he clearly doesn't know my Libby.

Sitting beside her after the doctor leaves, I say, "Well, you've caused quite a stir, Miss Jordan." Then I laugh. "Thank goodness you don't have a concussion, baby."

"That beautiful dream was worth it, Jaclyn. You always glow, but in my dream, you were enveloped in a radiant light. I know that when I die, you'll be right there for me, and you'll say, "Yes, Libby. I am indeed your guardian angel, baby."

"Oh, Libby. What has that dream done to you? You seem lighter and freer, baby."

Libby draws me close and holds me. "The love I felt from you was immeasurable, Jaclyn. I feel it here with you now, but your love was completely ethereal in my dream."

The doctor ordered Libby to rest for at least twenty-four hours, and I'm going to make sure she follows his orders. "Baby, I'm going get us a few groceries, and pick up a bottle of wine. We'll cook dinner here tonight."

"I want to go with you, Jaclyn. You haven't been out of my sight for over a week, and I don't want to be apart from you."

As I place a pillow behind her head and tuck her into the couch with a throw blanket, I say, "Oh Libby, my love, you're such a sweetheart."

"Libby, we have a full week here or longer if we wish." Kissing her lips and knot on her forehead, I say, "You stay right here, baby. I won't be long." She nods but looks deflated.

As I walk out into the crisp afternoon to the grocery store, I suddenly miss her. Smiling to myself, I realize that Libby and I have fallen in love all over again. Walking back into the cottage with two bags of groceries, I see Libby sound asleep right where I left her. Setting the groceries on the kitchen table, I walk quietly to the couch and gaze at her. That knot on her head pains me, but her peaceful expression makes me smile.

As I continue to gaze at her, I can't seem to look away. It's hard to believe she came back to me after all these years. I suppose she truly did love me all this time, just as she promised. Smiling, I return to the kitchen and I hear her say, "Hi, beautiful."

"Well, hello, baby," I say, as I walk back and sit on the edge of the sofa beside her.

"Did you miss me?" she asks.

Leaning down, I kiss her sweet lips tenderly, pull away slightly, and ask, "What do you think?"

Libby giggles and says, "Good, I missed you too."

"How do you feel?"

"Better. The pain pill helped, but I feel a bit loopy."

"Well, you just lay here and rest. I'm going to make that salad again—the one you inhaled the first day I fed you."

"Yum, that was a good salad." Libby says, settling in as I tuck the cover in more and smile at her. She says, "Come close, Jaclyn, I have something to say."

Leaning in, I ask, "And what is that, baby?"

As I gaze at her, I can tell the pain pill has made her a bit loopy, but I smile, waiting for her to speak.

She giggles, then, with her eyes closed, whispers, "I realized on the trip down that I'm still so in love with you, Jaclyn." She giggles again, then dozes off.

Feeling a lump in my throat, I smile at my beautiful Libby. I touch her cheek and whisper, "Thank you, God, for bringing her home to me."

Libby is still asleep as I set the table on the back deck of our cottage. Gazing out, I see the waves are still churning from the storm. It feels cool outside, but we can wear sweaters while dining.

Kissing my love on the lips, she wakes, smiles at me, and asks, "Are you my guardian angel?"

Kneeling beside her, I whisper, "Yes, baby, I am."

She whispers, "But you're my lover too."

I whisper, "Yes, Libby, I am indeed your lover." Then I kiss her deeply as I feel my feminine core burn with desire. Feeling her arms pull me close, I kiss her passionately and feel her hunger for me.

She pulls away slightly and whispers, "Damn, this bump," followed by a playful growl.

Laughing, I say, "Dinner is on the deck, baby. Are you hungry?"

"Yes, but not for food."

Smiling at her, I say, "Me too. Let's give it another day to heal, okay?"

As I pour our wine, I look at Libby and wink, "You look better, baby. The nap did you some good." I kiss her knot softly. "Does it still hurt?"

"Somewhat, but I'll be fine by tomorrow." Looking at me, she says, "I love cuddling, Jaclyn, but I'm ready for much more."

Laughing, I say, "Well, we will see how you are tomorrow, baby."

"Oh, Jaclyn, I'd wait another nine years for you if I had to. I'm just being a bit dramatic."

We bring our glasses together, and I whisper, "This is our second chance, baby."

Libby smiles sweetly and nods; her eyes glisten with emotion as she gently taps her glass against mine.

The afternoon breeze blows gently across the deck, sending a chill through the air. "It's a bit chilly, isn't it," I ask, feeling the coolness on my skin.

"Yes, but it's waking me up. I'm not going to take another pill unless the pain becomes unbearable. I don't want to sleep for two days—I have other things in mind." Libby says with a playful wink.

Laughing, I say, "Hmmm, I think you have the same

sexual appetite that you had nine years ago, and something tells me it has increased."

Libby laughs and asks, "And what gives you that impression?"

"Because I know you, Libby Jordan." I laugh and ask, "Am I going to be able to handle you now?"

"I believe you'll handle me just fine. After all, I remember your sexual appetite was pretty high, too."

"Oh, Libby, we are going to have to stop this. Your knot needs at least another day to hea."

"I know," Libby says with a playful growl. She looks at me and asks, "Well, can we at least take a walk on the beach?"

Looking at her knot closely and then into her eyes, I softly say, "Well, I don't think a short walk would hurt. So yes."

Libby stands, picks up our dishes, and then says, "Good. At least I can hold your hand while we walk." I shake my head and laugh.

As Libby and I walk on the beach, we take turns tossing Poppy her ball. We laugh at her as she chases it with boundless energy. "I think the little girl is happy to be back on dry land," I say.

"Go get it, Poppy!" Libby exclaims, giving the ball a gentle toss.

"I love watching you and Poppy play ball, Libby. You're both my girls, you know."

Libby stops, looks at me, and says, "You and I are so much more, Jaclyn. But I told you days ago, I would always be your girl."

"Yes, you did, and you always will, Libby."

CHAPTER FIFTEEN: LIBBY

The morning light streaming through the open bedroom doors wakes me early at our beach cottage. As I lie with Jaclyn in my arms, I listen to the waves breaking on the shore just outside our door.

Last night, we took another walk on the beach, showered, and went to bed early. We drifted off late in the night after a few hours of cuddling and talking. Rising gently so as not to wake Jaclyn, I ease out of bed, walk to the door, lean against the casing, and gaze out at the water. It's a beautiful and cool morning; the water is much calmer today. It gently laps onto the shore as if completely exhausted from yesterday's storm.

Touching my head, I can tell the knot is almost gone, but it's still tender. As I look at Jaclyn, my erotic love for her begins to stir, and I ache with a longing to know her intimately again. I ache for her and don't want to wait any longer.

Undressing to join her completely nude, I stand beside the bed, admiring her beauty. She awakens, looks at me surprised, she whispers, "Libby."

She moves to the edge of the bed, draws me to her, and says, "Libby, baby, look at you. You're even more beautiful now."

Gazing down at her, I thread my fingers through her dark hair and gaze at her with intense longing. "I want you, Jaclyn."

She nods, smiles, and begins to ask, "How is your…"

I touch her lips with my index finger and whisper, "I'm fine. I'm just very hungry."She smiles at me and then stands. "Okay, Libby. I'm famished for you, baby."

Jaclyn begins to unbutton her pajama top as I stand, gazing at her, waiting patiently for her to reveal her beauty to me. I long to see my lover again, to feel her warmth, to taste her sweetness. Watching her undress for me is intoxicating, and I remain where I am, savoring every moment of her revealing beauty.

"You're still so gorgeous, Jaclyn. You always took my breath away, and now, even more. My god, how I love your body."

Jaclyn closes the doors, then gracefully walks back to me, pulling me close. "I've ached for you too, Libby. your nude body is so familiar yet so very different. My gosh, the years have been very good to you. You're much the same baby, but now, you're like a goddess."

Smiling at her I whisper, "You always did know how to talk to me in the bedroom, Mrs. Clarkson."

"I did, huh?" She asks as she pulls me to her and grins.

Nodding at her, I say, "You know you did, and still do, beautiful."

Holding me close, she softly says, "I believe I need to upgrade your name from baby to Goddess. What do you think of that?"

Feeling her warm body against mine, I whisper, "Call me

whatever you wish, as long as you promise to be my lover forever."

Jaclyn grins then kisses my lips tenderly. "Libby, I do indeed promise to be your lover forever. Nothing will ever keep me from you again."

"Lay next to me, Jaclyn," I say, kissing her cheek and gently holding her hand.

We return to our warm bed, pull one another close, and gaze into each other's souls. "Do you feel that, Libby?"

"Of course I feel it, Jaclyn. I've felt it since I first laid eyes on you, but now it's more sensual and erotic."

"Miss Jordan, I do believe this is going to be a very lovely day," she says, pulling me so close our faces are just inches apart, then kisses me softly. As I move my fingers through her dark hair, I open my lips and feel her tenderness as our tongues swirl and dance.

Jaclyn reaches around me and rakes her nails tenderly across my ass. I giggle, knowing she remembers how much I loved that so many moons ago. I pull away, smile at her, and laugh again. She asks sweetly, "Why did you always love that so much, Libby?"

Closing my eyes, I feel the familiar goosebumps traveling across my nude body as she continues, "Because you were always such a woman to me, Jaclyn, and I love your beautiful hands.

Opening my eyes, I feel Jaclyn's perfect fingers touch my lips, tracing their outline. "You're rendering me completely helpless, Jaclyn."

"Good, because I wish to take you first, my lovely Goddess."

"Well, that wasn't my plan, but I won't fight you, considering I'm wounded." Jaclyn laughs, then playfully spanks my ass.

"God, how I've missed you, Libby. I just want to lie here and hold you close. Would you like that, baby?" Nodding in agreement, I gaze into her eyes and see the depth of her love for me.

I feel as though we are two lost lovers sailing across a vast, endless ocean lost in time. Lost together after the universe tried to sever our love years ago. But our love was, and is, too grand for the expanse of time to keep us apart.

"I've never stopped loving you, Libby, and I'm still so in love with you now."

Touching her cheek, I whisper, "I know, Jaclyn, and I am deeply in love with you."Well, you're back where you belong, right here in my arms again, baby," Jaclyn says, rising and looking down at me with those dark, loving eyes. She touches my breast and moves her thumb lightly across my nipple. She lays back on her side and begins to move to my breast, whispering, "I want to taste you, baby."

Still wrapped together closely I watch her move to my breasts. She kisses them and then takes one of my nipples into her mouth. I feel her warm tongue swirl over it. "You taste like my Libby," she whispers, as she begins to suck each of my nipples tenderly.

My fingers are intertwined in her soft brown hair as I watch her mouth on my nipples. "That feels so good, Jaclyn."

She pulls away for a moment, gazes at me, and whispers, "You've always had the loveliest nipples. I'm enjoying loving them again."

Closing my eyes, I give in entirely to Jaclyn's love. She's taking her time with me just as she used to. Jaclyn never rushed our lovemaking. Now, I fully appreciate her willingness to be tender and not rush.

"You're an amazing lover, Jaclyn; you always were," I tell her as I continue watching her love me. She moves to my stomach, kissing it with the same tender passion she gave my nipples. My god, she's absolutely incredible.

She pulls me tight against her face as she kisses and licks my tummy, raking her nails over my ass again as she continues licking me. "Oh god, Jaclyn, I could almost come for you now."

She looks up at me, softly saying, "You better relax, Libby, because I don't intend to let you orgasm any time soon. You're home again, and I'm going to take my time with you."

"Oh, Jaclyn."

"Lay on your tummy, baby."

Rolling onto my tummy, I melt into the bedding, as Jaclyn continues loving me. She moves onto my back with her sensual, warm body. "Your breasts feel incredible on me, Jaclyn. My god, woman, you're driving me mad."

She laughs lightly in my ear and says, "We still have all day, my young Goddess; and the day is still young." She kisses my shoulders, biting them playfully, as I giggle at her. She then moves to my back, licking it with the long, loving strokes that I remember so well.

I'm helpless to do anything but enjoy her, letting her take me as she wishes. I remember when she's like this, she could love me for hours. "Your hard nipples feel erotic as hell against my ass, Jaclyn." She rises and brushes her nipples lightly across my ass. I begin to moan, encouraging her to continue.

"Jaclyn, honey, this is torture."

"Torture?" She asks as she continues raking her nipples against my ass.

"Yes, torture, woman," I say in jest.

As she continues she says, with a teasing smile, "I don't remember you protesting like this years ago. Why now?"

Laughing, I say, "I'm not. I'm loving this."

"That's more like it, my sweet Goddess." She says as she moves her mouth to my ass. She then licks it and bites it just as she did with my shoulders. She rakes her sexy nails across my ass once again, sending chills rapidly throughout my whole body.

"I've always loved your ass, Libby." She says, as she grabs it. "So full and sexy. I have to say, when you came back to me, you returned completely ripe, baby."

Laughing into the bedding, I reply, "Ripe? You're too much, Jaclyn."

Jaclyn laughs, too, as we both get tickled by the moment. I roll over, and she returns to my face; and we giggle together for a moment. "I'm enjoying your lovemaking, Jaclyn. I'm all yours, beautiful."

"Yes, you are, baby," she says while gazing into my eyes. As she lies on top of me I feel her mature bosoms and womanness. I shudder at the intensity of her mature erotic body against mine. Our mouths meet and the passion ignites. Our appetite for one another demands to be fed. Our zealous kisses are untamed and wild as we feed one another savagely. Jaclyn pulls away, looking at me as she says, "God, how I've missed you."

Grabbing Jaclyn's hair, I say, "I'm a mature and hungry woman now, Jaclyn. There's no need to be tender any longer. Show me the passion you have for me."

Jaclyn stares at me for a moment, and then her dark eyes turn provocative and wild. She grabs me with complete rawness and we begin to fight the past, angry at time for keeping us apart. I grab her hair, pulling her to me as our mouths feed on each other. We are both starved for each other's affection, yearning for the closeness we've missed all these years apart.

"My god, Libby. I will never let you get away from me again," she says before our mouths and tongues meet again.

Jaclyn pulls away, moving her hand between my legs as I open them for her.

"You're completely drenched, baby." Jaclyn gathers my liquid, entering me as she gazes into my soul.

"Yes, please take me, make me yours again, Jaclyn."

She pushes deeply into me as I whimper and moan. Jaclyn keeps her eyes on me as she loves me with the complete rawness and the passion I asked for. She thrusts deeply into my sensual core. I wonder, is this the same Jaclyn from years ago? No, this is the Jaclyn of my future, not my past—the one I need now, and she is giving me everything I desire.

Jaclyn is deep inside me, penetrating my walls with a fierceness I've never known. I gaze at her; she feels almost like a stranger to me, but I know it's her, so I relax completely, allowing her to totally consume me.

"Deeper," I whisper. Jaclyn looks at me, her eyes darting back and forth into my eyes. She pushes deeper with loving force.

"Libby," she whispers as she gives me all her strength. I feel my walls begin to cave, I close my eyes, and enjoy this beautiful, erotic ride. Opening my eyes, I meet her gaze, and smile. She knows I'm ready. She pulls out gently, moving to my clit, and begins moving her fingers firmly against it.

I feel myself peaking. I touch Jaclyn's face, gaze into her heart, and feel her love. I let go, releasing myself to her. "I'm yours, Jaclyn," I say as I begin to climax. The orgasm is intense, loving, and uncontrolled. I moan and cry out. "Jaclyn!"

"Yes, baby." She says as she watches me climax. With locked eyes, we share this moment—beautiful, raw, and tender.

As my orgasm abates, I feel a rush of vulnerability, but also her intense love for me. I smile at my future, my lover. Closing my eyes, I pull her close; I need her arms around me.

"Hold me, Jaclyn." She wraps her entire body around me, pulling me close with an all-encompassing love.

"I've loved you forever, Libby." She holds me against her warm body, and I relax, letting her love me.

Laying in Jaclyn's arms, I savor the most beautiful orgasm I've had since she released me years ago.

CHAPTER SIXTEEN: JACLYN

Holding Libby closely, I feel her perfect love enveloping me. "Thank you for coming home to me, baby," I say, hugging her lovingly.

"I had little choice, my heart needed you. It's been so broken without you."

I rise above Libby and gaze into her sweet eyes, whispering, "I never meant to hurt you, baby, you know that."

Nodding, with a smile, she says, "Yes, Jaclyn, I know."

"All I've ever wanted is what was best for you, Libby."

"And what's best for me now, Jaclyn?" She asks, as she gazes into my eyes.

"Living your life with me, Libby—that's what's best for you now."

"Yes, it is, and I'm what's best for you, Jaclyn."

"Yes, you are," I whisper, as I suck on her earlobe seductively, whispering, "I have yet to taste your sweet nectar, baby. May I?"

"You may taste any part of me you wish, Jaclyn."

"I've smelled Libby throughout our intense lovemaking, but I want her on my lips, tongue, and mouth. Kissing her tummy again, I go lower and inhale her seductive sex. She still smells much the same, however, now she is sweetly ripe and erotically mature. My core burns with pain as I dip my tongue into her river. It's flooded with sweet nectar from her orgasm. All I want is to drink her in and swallow her.

Gazing up at her, I whisper, "You even taste like a Goddess."

Moving closer, I lick and swallow every ounce of her sweetness, sucking her clit as it swells again for me. I move my tongue across the top, remembering what she likes. She whispers, "Yes, Jaclyn."

Entering her again, I gaze at her, watching how she responds and seeing her lovely green eyes on me. Giving her tender thrusts, I move my tongue back and forth over the top of her clit, increasing the pressure with my tongue and the tempo of my thrusts. My mouth and fingers are in sync as I continue loving her.

"Jaclyn," she whimpers. I feel her getting close. As she squeezes my fingers tightly, I keep the same rhythm. Suddenly, I feel her. She's ready to lose herself to me again, she cries out, "Jaclyn, I'm coming!"

Smiling, I continue—making my beautiful young Goddess orgasm over and over.

Gently removing my fingers, I suck her clit one last time, entirely for my own enjoyment.

Moving to her lovely face, I smile as she touches my face lightly with her fingers. "You're still such a giving lover, Jaclyn." She puts her arms around me and pulls me close.

"You still taste heavenly, Libby. I've never forgotten your taste and scent, baby."

I move off of Libby, pulling her into my arms, as I whisper, "Rest, baby. We have all day." Holding her close, I feel her slip off into a sweet slumber. Knowing she can't hear me, I whisper tearfully, "Thank you for coming home to me, Libby.

The pain I've endured without you in my life has been pure hell."

~

I wake to feel Libby kissing my breast, "Hi, baby. That feels incredible."

She continues loving my nipple and as she says, "I hope it's okay that I woke you?"

Laughing softly, I say, "I would've hated to sleep through this." Libby giggles and then begins to suck my erect nipples. "It feels so good having you make love to me again." I relax, and surrender to her.

She holds my bosoms in her hands, pushing them together as she licks my nipples with the bottom of her tongue as she gazes at me. She takes a nipple in her warm mouth and then winks at me. I shudder with chills as I continue to watch her loving me. Libby is sucking my nipples harder; knowing I love it like this.

"Yes, Libby."

She moves to my sexual haven and begins smelling me. I watch her closely as she inhales my scent. I'm aching for her to dip her tongue into my core. I want to watch her swallow me.

Whispering, "Libby? Will you swallow me like you used to?"

She winks seductively at me, giving me a wicked grin. My gosh, Libby is indeed a woman! She is taking me with such aggressive seductiveness.

She moves to my gateway, scoops up my nectar with her soft tongue, as she looks at me, and swallows. She does this again and again as I watch.

"I love watching you do that, Libby."

"You taste incredible, Jaclyn." She quickly dips in for

another taste, gathering more of my liquid in her mouth. She then crawls up my body slowly with my elixir in her mouth.

As she approaches my face, our eyes meet, and instinctively, I understand her desire. I open my mouth and Libby follows suit, letting the nectar drip into my mouth, her eyes locking with mine, utterly seducing me.

Pulling her to my lips, I taste my essence on her mouth as we kiss breathlessly. Breaking our kiss, I look into her soul. "Libby, this is almost too much, baby."

She kisses my cheek tenderly. "Jaclyn, it's me, beautiful," she says and she looks into my eyes and smiles. Touching her face, I bring Libby back to my lips giving into my erotic craving for her. Our tongues reunite. Hungrily feeding each other again.

Libby moves to my clit and glides her tongue across it with intense pressure. "Oh, Libby, I'm going to come if you don't stop."

"Well, I'm not ready for you to come yet," She says as she crawls seductively up my body again. Her face reaches mine, and she whispers, "I want this incredible body of yours to ache for me a little longer. It will make your orgasms more intense, beautiful."

"Oh, god, Libby, I'm already in pain."

"I know my lover, but I'm not ready for you to orgasm, so you'll just have to wait. Won't you?" She licks my lips and sucks them softly.

"My god, Libby. Who are you?"

"Your lover, Jaclyn. I have a serious question that I need you to answer for me."

Gazing at her, I pull her face to me and say, "Ask me anything."

Seductively she asks, "Miss Clarkson, would you like for me to take you like I used to?"

Looking at her I whisper, "Yes."

"I thought you might," She says then gives me a wicked grin.

Libby slides off the bed and says, "Come here, lover, let me take care of you."

"Oh god, Libby. You have indeed grown up."

CHAPTER SEVENTEEN: LIBBY

Jaclyn moves to the edge of the bed and remains on her knees with her back toward me. I grip her shoulders tenderly and pull her closer. She pulls her hair to one side and looks back at me. "Take me, Libby. I'm aching for you."

Feeling her mound against mine, I begin to rub her ass like I used to. She lays her head on the bed and moans. "I haven't forgotten what you like, Jaclyn."

"No you haven't, Libby, and you're driving me mad."

"Good, that's what I should be doing."

Still rubbing her ass with my left hand, I gather some of her liquid, then I enter her sanctuary. I push in slowly as I grab her back and hips with my arm. "Do you like this, Jaclyn?"

She whimpers and says, "You know I do."

As I plunge into her depths, I begin to rock her like I did on *Paper-Moon* days ago. Jaclyn pushes back with each thrust. Gazing at her beautiful body, I increase the tempo, and she meets them with intense force, moving in rhythm with me.

"Libby?!"

"Yes, Jaclyn?"

"Oh, Libby," She whispers breathlessly.

Continuing to thrust deep inside her, we move together as one, rocking together with one goal—to let this incredible woman know who she belongs to. "I love you submissive like this, Jaclyn."

"Oh, Libby" I'm emotionally and erotically in pain for you, baby."

"I know, relax, lover," I whisper as I continue pleasing her.

Jaclyn feels so good against me; she is the most beautiful woman I've ever known. How I won this woman's heart is a mystery, but she loves and desires me; this much I know.

"How does this feel, beautiful?"

"Oh, Libby, you know exactly how it feels and what you're doing to me, baby."

I smile because I remember how much I loved pleasing her this way, and I still do.

"Libby?"

"Yes?" I answer as I keep my thrusts at a tender but steady tempo.

"Give me more, baby, please."

Increasing my force, I push and thrust much deeper, even more than I believe she expected. "Oh, Libby."

It wasn't a protest so I continue at the same pace and rhythm, enjoying every minute. "Like you said, we have all day, beautiful. I hope you're comfortable because I plan to keep you like this for a while."

"Oh damn, Libby." Jaclyn raises her head from the bed, then looks back at me and says, "Yes, Libby. Keep fucking me, baby."

Plunging deeper, I begin to rock Jaclyn intensely. She lets out a moaning cry that I don't recognize, but I sure as hell love it. "Like this, beautiful?"

"Oh, Libby, yes, baby."

I spank her ass and continue loving my woman hard and intensely. "Libby?!'

"Yes?"

"You've never spanked me before."

I spank her harder and ask, "Do you like it?"

Jacklyn bucks back against me and says, "Oh, Libby, yes, I love it."

Our rhythm increases, and I sense Jaclyn is ready to release, I reach under and touch her clit. I've never felt her this engorged. "I believe you might be ready, Mrs. Clarkson. Are you?"

"Libby, you are so bad. You're enjoying this as much as I am, aren't you?"

"You mean watching you on your knees submissive to me?"

"Yes! She breathlessly says.

"It's quite erotic, I must admit. Are you ready to come, beautiful?" I ask as I spank her again.

She whispers, "Oh, Libby, those spankings are delightfully wicked. Spank me again, baby?"

"Well, I don't know, lover. Will you be a good girl and come for me?"

"Libby! My god, who are you?! Yes, I'll be good, I'll come for you if you spank me more."

"You mean like this? I ask as I spank her sweet, tight ass harder.

"Baby! I've never felt this erotically helpless, but I love this from you."

" Are you ready, beautiful?"

"Yes, Libby. I'm so ready to come for you, baby."

Jaclyn rises, and I pull her to me. Her back is against my breast, and my mouth is at her ear. Reaching around, my hand moves to her swollen clit, touching it lightly. "Oh, Libby, It's been so long since you took me like this."

Gently gripping her breast, I hold her tighter against my body and begin moving my fingers in a circular motion.

"You're even stronger now, baby."

"Come for me, beautiful. I want to feel you tumble and fall."

Jaclyn whimpers. I hold her tight, increasing the pressure. As her body trembles, I whisper, "I love you, Jaclyn." She moans softly, as she surrenders in my arms. "Yes, come for me, beautiful."

"Libby..." She cries out. I feel her falling. "I'm coming, baby."

I continue loving her, feeling her climax again and again. Even when she thinks she can't come again, I give her another orgasm to show her that she can. "That's all, Libby."

"Jaclyn, please turn towards me." She turns, and our faces are separated by mere inches, drawing us into an intimate closeness. I reach for her sex, then pull away a bit so I can watch her, and gather more liquid from her. Staring into her dark, loving eyes, I begin touching her as before and watch her fall again. She whispers, "Libby.... baby."

"You're mine, Jaclyn, you always have been," I say as she orgasms sweetly one last time.

"Come here, Jaclyn," I say as I take her hand, gently pulling her onto the bed. Drawing her to me, and holding her close as I kiss her lips.

"Oh, Libby, how I've missed you. My gosh, that was fucking incredible."

"You're an amazing lover, Jaclyn, but we've always been hot in the bedroom, if I remember correctly."

Jaclyn rises, looks at me, and grins. "Your memory is correct, baby. You were always aggressive in bed, Libby, but honey, It's going to take me a while to get used to 'This Libby.'"

"I wasn't too forceful, was I?"

Laughing, she touches my lips with her fingertips, as she says, "Let's just say I want more of this Libby."

Pulling her close, I look at her and grin. "I'll give you whatever you need."

She traces my lips with her fingertips and says, "I love you so much."

"I love you, Jaclyn. I've never stopped."

CHAPTER EIGHTEEN: JACLYN

W alking down Duval Street with my arm looped through Libby's, I glance at her and wink. She grins and asks, "What are you thinking about, beautiful?"

Gazing at her, I say, "I'm thinking about how magical these past couple of weeks with you have been."

"They've been incredible, Jaclyn."

We continue walking and occasionally stopping to browse the shops along the way. "Are you hungry, baby?"

"Yes,where should we have lunch?"

Pointing across the street at a charming café, I say, "That place looks like it might be good. Let's go there."

Sitting at an outside table, I order a bottle of chardonnay. "It's crisp today. Are you cold, love?

"No, Jaclyn. I'm fine. You still enjoy fussing over me," she says with a grin.

"Does it bother you, Libby?"

She grins and says, "It could never bother me."

"I know you're not my eighteen-year-old Libby anymore,

but sometimes I still see her. Even after all these years, I still feel protective of you."

"Jaclyn, I feel very protective of you now, so I understand. I suppose I did years ago, as well, but now, I'm extremely protective of you."

Nodding, I say, "Yes, Libby, you are. I felt it the whole trip down, especially during the storm.

After I taste our wine for approval, our waiter pours us each a glass. We clink our glasses together, and Libby whispers sweetly, "To our second chance, Jaclyn."

We sit quietly, sipping our wine and occasionally stealing glances at one another. "This wine is delicious. I think I'll get us a bottle to enjoy later today."

"That would be lovely, Jaclyn."

"Libby. I feel like we're on our honeymoon. Does that sound silly?"

She reaches for my hand, our fingers immediately intertwining as she gazes at me. "No, Jaclyn, it does feel like that. I think it's romantic and quite accurate."

"Accurate?" I asked.

Libby continues looking at me but remains silent. What is she saying? Perhaps I should nod and sip my wine, but I can't. "What are you saying, Libby?"

"Jaclyn, you know what I'm saying," she says as she continues gazing into my eyes.

"Libby, let's take this conversation to the cottage. Okay?"

She nods at me, remaining sincere with her gaze.

As we leave the café, we continue walking Duval Street and then return to our cottage a couple of blocks over. Opening the cottage's French doors, Libby and I sit on the wooden deck overlooking the water.

The mood during our walk was quiet but filled with tender anticipation. As we sit at the outdoor table, Libby pours us another glass of wine. After a moment of silence, I feel compelled to speak first. "Are you coming home to me for good, Libby?"

She reaches for me, tucking a strand of hair behind my ear, and says, "Jaclyn, I've been home for good this entire trip."

"Libby, it may seem glaringly obvious to you, but I can't make any assumptions. I need you to tell me what you want."

"Oh, Jaclyn, you can't possibly think I want to stay in Jacksonville. We've toasted our second chance the whole trip. Haven't we?"

"Yes, we have, Libby."

"Jaclyn, I want to be with you for the rest of my life. However, I left all those years ago because you sent me away. I need you to tell me what you want. If you want me to stay, that's something that needs to come from you."

Gazing at the water, I sip my wine, contemplating her words. Libby is right;. she left because I ended things. I should be the one to ask her to stay. Why is it so hard to ask her this?

Closing my eyes, I recall snippets of our trip sailing across the Atlantic. Libby at the helm, us laughing and playing gin, and battling the storm. The beautiful moments from the past two weeks glide across my mind, making me smile.

Opening my eyes, I look at Libby and see my future. "You're right, Libby. We didn't toast second chances just for the hell of it. We've made loving declarations not only during our intimate moments, but throughout our time together."

Libby smiles at me and nods in silence.

Feeling altogether nervous, I reach for her and touch her cheek tenderly. "Libby, I want you to come home to me permanently. I want *Paper-Moon* moored at my dock indefinitely, and I want you to live with me, baby. Please share my home and life. I want to care for you for the rest of my life. Will you live with me forever, Libby?"

Tears stream down Libby's cheeks, so I pull her close and kiss them away. She whispers, "That's all I've ever wanted, Jaclyn. You have always been home to me, and I want to spend my life with you. Yes, Jaclyn, I would love to live with you and share our lives."

Rising, I climb into Libby's lap and wrap my arms around her neck, still holding my wine glass. Hugging her tightly, I gaze at the water and smile. "Oh, god, Libby, you make me so incredibly happy. You have no idea what you do to me."

Pulling away, Libby gives me a broad smile and says, "It's about time you came to your senses, beautiful."

My head falls back as I laugh loudly. "Oh, Libby, baby. You're my everything!"

She draws me close, sits her glass on the table, and hugs me with what seems like every ounce of strength she has. "I love you, Jaclyn."

Kissing her cheek, I let her hold me tightly as I dream about our future.

"You've made me the happiest woman on this earth, Libby." Pulling away, I look at her, smile, and kiss her lips sweetly. "You don't even have to worry about work anytime soon, if at all, baby."

"Jaclyn, are you asking me to be your 'kept woman?'"

Laughing, I nod and seductively say, "Yes, I am. That way, we could sail every day and make love all night. What ya think?"

Libby laughs loudly, then looks into my eyes. "I'll take you up on that for about a month, but you and I both know I need my work."

"Of course, baby, but I'm going to hold you to that month. And that time doesn't start until we return to Savannah, just so you know, young lady."

Libby holds me in her lap and says, "Finally, you're mine, Jaclyn Clarkson. You always have been, but now it's official."

Setting my wine glass down, I begin tracing the outline of her lips with my index finger; I look into her lovely green eyes and say, "Yes, baby. It's official, and nothing will ever keep us apart again."

Libby bites my index finger gently, then sucks it into her mouth. Our eyes lock as she begins sucking it slowly and seductively. "Oh, Libby."

As I straddle Libby, she slips her soft hand under my dress and begins caressing my legs. As I close my eyes, she starts touching me through my panties.

"These have to come off," She whispers.

Rising while still in her lap, she slowly pulls them down just enough to reach me. "Are you wet for me, Miss Clarkson?"

I nod and say, "Yes."

"Are you sure?" She asks provocatively.

"You know I am; you're just being naughty."

"Maybe, but I need to be sure. Don't you think?"

"Yes, Miss Jordan, I do believe you're right." Moving to her lips, I whisper, "Go ahead and check to be sure if you'd like."

As Libby touches me, I moan into her mouth. Obviously, I am very wet because Libby begins to rub my clit with her slick thumb.

"Libby, that feels amazing."

As our mouths love one another, Libby enters me gently and pulls me to herself as she leans back. I begin to rock against her fingers deep inside me. We find a loving rhythm and ride it together. "You're mine, Jaclyn."

"Yes, I am," I say breathlessly.

As our mouths and tongues greedily feed one another, I begin to fall. Libby increases the rhythm; she knows I'm coming. Moaning helplessly, I orgasm as Libby grips the back of my hair, holding me tightly. "Yes, baby."

"Jaclyn," She simply whispers.

Libby pulls out gently and draws me to herself once more. She begins loving me with her whole body. "Libby, I'll love you forever, baby. You will never know a day without my love."

CHAPTER NINETEEN: LIBBY

Opening our cottage's small oven, I peek in to check on our Thanksgiving turkey. It's well on its way but still needs about two more hours.

"Libby, that turkey looks divine. I'm glad you're in charge of it."

"Mama and I always cooked together on Thanksgiving morning. She taught me to cook from an early age. That reminds me, could you turn on the radio, Jaclyn? The Macy's parade is on. We can't cook Thanksgiving dinner without listening to the Macy's parade."

Jaclyn laughs, "Yes, let me see if I can find it."

Watching Jaclyn turn the dials to find the station, I walk behind her, wrap my arms around her waist, and hug her. "Here it is, Libby."

"Yay, you found it!"

Jaclyn turns around and gazes at me. "I love seeing you happy, baby."

"I'm incredibly happy."

"You want to know something I've noticed over the last week or more, Libby?" Smiling at her, I ask, "What?"

Taking my left hand between hers, she says, "It's something I am truly thankful for this Thanksgiving, Libby—your hand, baby. I haven't seen you clench it in over a week."

"You're right, Jaclyn," I say, glancing at it between her loving hands. "Perhaps it just needs your love."

Jaclyn kisses it tenderly as she looks at me, then smiles with her gentle dark eyes.

Walking to the radio, I turn the dial, and Jaclyn looks at me puzzled. I wink at her as the dial finds a slow ballad. Etta James begins singing *Someone to Watch Over Me.* "Will you dance with me, Miss Clarkson?"

"Yes, Miss Jordan. I will indeed dance with you."

In the living area of our love cottage, Jaclyn and I begin to dance slowly. With one hand resting on her back and the other cradling hers, our bodies move together smoothly. Finding my rhythm with Jaclyn comes so easily, and we find it immediately as we begin dancing. "I love how perfect it feels holding you, Jaclyn."

Holding Jaclyn close, we dance for the next hour or so. We move slowly and deliberately, our bodies in sync with the music and each other, enjoying this tender moment together.

"I'm loving this, Libby, but perhaps we should check on Thanksgiving dinner."

"You are my Thanksgiving dinner, Jaclyn. I cooked the turkey just for the hell of it."

Roaring with laughter, Jaclyn pulls away, takes my hand, and says, "Come in this kitchen with me. I have to finish the cornbread dressing while you check your turkey."

I slap her ass and say, "Well, you'll be my dessert then."

"Libby! Don't start spanking me again, or this Thanksgiving dinner won't happen at all."

"You like that, don't you, beautiful?"

"We're not going to discuss it either, Miss Jordan. You've

discovered my weakness, and I can't even imagine what it will be like to live with you."

"I'll play nice, beautiful," I say as I wink at her.

Jaclyn shakes her head, smiles, and then giggles.

"I enjoy seeing you a little shy, and hearing you giggle. It makes my heart melt."

She walks to me and wraps her arms around me, staying silent. I pull her close, closing my eyes as I hold her tightly, then kiss her cheek softly. "Let's finish our cooking. Okay?" She kisses my lips tenderly and nods.

"Everything looks so delicious, Libby. Are you ready to eat, baby?"

"Yes, but we should say grace, Jaclyn. We must thank our creator for bringing us back together."

Jaclyn smiles and nods, then begins saying our Thanksgiving grace while holding my hand. As I listen to her prayer, I feel her immense love for me, and I'm overcome with thankfulness.

"That was beautiful, Jaclyn. Thank you, and Happy Thanksgiving, my love."

"Happy Thanksgiving, Libby."

It's late at night as Jaclyn and I walk on the beach with Poppy. "This is the first Thanksgiving since Mama died that I haven't felt sad, Jaclyn."

"I'm glad, Libby. Your mother was wonderful; no wonder you grieved her for so long, baby."

"Where have you spent the last few Thanksgivings, Jaclyn?"

"Well, I spent them with friends and my sister in Virginia. Last year, though, I spent it alone."

"Alone? Was that hard?"

"Not really, Libby. You know my parents died years ago, and I was young to lose them, but I got through it okay. I've just been alone since then; I don't see my sister, Elizabeth, that much. She has her own family."

"Well, you will never have another holiday alone, Jaclyn."

"And you'll never have another sad one, Libby. Not if I can help it, baby."

We continue walking and playing ball with Poppy, watching the moonlight dance on the waves. Holding hands, I feel the cool east breeze blowing through my hair and the love we share.

"When should we return home, Jaclyn?" I ask as we continue walking.

"Never, Libby," she replies, looking at me sincerely.

Stopping our walk, I pull her close and ask, "So, you wish to make this a perpetual honeymoon?"

Jaclyn touches my face and says, "That sounds like heaven, Libby." We continue walking, then she says, "Maybe in a couple of days, baby. Is that okay with you?"

"Yes, that's fine. It will be sad to leave, but we have a whole life to live and many plans and decisions to make. I look forward to the voyage home and living with you."

Libby, do you need to go back to Jacksonville for anything? If you do, I'll drive us. I don't want to wait for you to sail there and back. You're home now and agreed to live with me, so I'm keeping you.

Grinning, I say, "There's nothing I can't do by phone, but it might be best to go to Jacksonville and tell my editor about my decision to leave in person. And I'd love it if you drove me; I don't want you out of my sight either."

Jaclyn hugs me as we walk, her arms wrapped around me. I feel that lovely breeze again and realize how incredibly happy and thankful I am. The woman I've loved forever is by my side, and a whole life with her is just waiting to be lived.

CHAPTER TWENTY: JACLYN

L eaning against the casing of our bedroom's exterior French door, which opens to the ocean, I watch the peaceful water gently break upon the shore. Glancing at Libby, I can't help but smile. She's still asleep, and I hate to wake her. Instead, I savor this tranquil moment, admiring her nude body nestled comfortably on the bed covers.

After a late walk on the beach, we danced again to slow ballads on the radio. Our bodies moving in rhythm led us to the bedroom, where we made love well into the early morning.

Today, we are departing Key West, and it's a bittersweet mix of emotions. Gazing at Libby, I am reminded of that day years ago when she asked me to sail to Key West with her. Closing my eyes, I can see my eighteen-year-old Libby, earnestly as she pleaded, "Jaclyn, please sail with me to Key West. I promise to love you forever. Will you please come with me?"

Replaying that moment and her sincerity to me that day

on the *Paper-Moon* overwhelms and stirs my soul. She was so very sincere.

Walking to her, I gaze at her tranquil face as she sleeps. Sailing to Key West and our time at the beach cottage has brought her a serene peace.

I'm not sure what living with this beautiful young woman will be like, but I know it will be wonderful. Touching her hair lightly, I thread my fingers through it; I've always loved her blonde locks.

As I gaze at her, memories of the day we first made love aboard *Paper-Moon* come flooding back. I had driven to the marina, aware she was skipping numerous classes during her senior year.

It became clear to me how deeply the death of her mother had affected Libby. With no maternal figure in her life after that loss, I felt a strong urge to step in and fill that void. That's how it all began.

Libby never viewed me in a maternal light, and she made that very clear. As I walked along the dock to reach her boat that day, I climbed onboard and peered downward through the boat's hatch. I caught sight of her changing clothes. She looked up and asked, "Jaclyn, are you okay? What are you doing here?"

After a moment, I was down in the cabin, trying to reason with her about school as she continued changing clothes. She removed her top and stood before me, her beautiful breast exposed.

The months leading up to this were filled with tender moments between us as I taught her piano lessons. There were many lingering hugs and intimate glances. Suppressing my feelings for her was incredibly difficult, and I frequently found myself angry with myself because she was an eighteen-year-old who had lost her mother that year.

Libby was always adamant that she wasn't a girl but an

independent woman who lived alone on her sailboat. She was unique, unlike any other woman or girl I had ever known.

As she stood before me that day with her breasts exposed, and her arms extended as she gripped the top of the open hatch, staring at me with those piercing green eyes of hers. She took my breath away, and I fell instantly in love with her.

Gazing at me, she simply said, "Touch me, Jaclyn."

"Libby, I can't, baby."

"I know you want me, Jaclyn. Touch me, beautiful." She whispered.

My heart began to race as I stood gazing at her beautiful breasts, as she stood still, waiting for me to decide. Approaching her, I pulled her close with my eyes fixed on her perfect bosoms. Her nipples were erect as I brushed over them with my thumbs. Libby closed her eyes and sighed.

I realized what she desired from me and what I had been fighting. Libby opened her eyes, gazed at me, then pulled me to her breast. I shuddered when I took her in my mouth. Libby's sweet, unique charm had already bewitched me, but I was utterly entranced at that moment.

We sailed to a secluded inlet, and I gave in to my over-whelming desire for her. We made love for hours that day, experiencing something so pure and loving that I had never felt before. Libby was, and still is, the embodiment of pure goodness, and I fell utterly in love with her that day.

Libby opens her eyes, smiles and says, "Good morning, beautiful."

Sitting on the edge of the bed with our fingers interlaced, I say, "Good morning, baby."

"What time is it?"

"It doesn't matter. All that matters is that I'm so in love with you."

"Awww, Jaclyn. What's made you so sweetly romantic this morning?"

"I just woke up completely in love with the woman who took me out on her sailboat years ago and made love to me all day."

Libby gazes at me with a grin. "That day was magical—I seduced you."

"Call it what you will, Miss Jordan but I've never lived a more perfect day than that day."

"It was perfect, wasn't it?"

"Yes, Libby, it was indeed." I kiss her lips sweetly, then ask, "Should we finish packing and head out?"

Libby stands and draws me to her. "Thank you for sailing with me to Key West, Jaclyn. And I do indeed promise to love you forever."

～

Libby, Poppy, and I are back on *Paper-Moon,* setting sail away from the marina and Key West. It's a beautiful, crisp November day as we smile at one another.

"Are you ready to sail, Jaclyn?" She asks with a huge grin.

"Your excitement is infectious, Libby. Yes, I am ready to sail, baby. Today, I will hoist the sails, and then you can trim them however you like. Does that sound okay?"

"Of course, beautiful. I'll sit back here and gaze at you while you work the sails."

Smiling at her, I grin and say, "Libby, I truly believe you will love me forever." I then hoist the sails, after which Libby trims them taut. The wind fills the sails, and I hear the canvas pop. Smiling, I look at Libby and say, "Now we're sailing."

Poppy jumps in my lap, and I start to laugh. "I think that part unnerves her a bit."

"It's okay, Poppy," Libby says sweetly. "We are going home, and I'll be living with you and your Mama. Is that okay with you, girl?"

Unexpectedly, Poppy barks at Libby, and we exchange surprised glances before bursting into laughter.

Leaning back, I feel the November breeze from the Atlantic flow through my hair and my visions of our future together. I gaze up at the 'JACLYN' flag and grin.

Closing my eyes, I continue to feel gratitude for this Thanksgiving week. I whisper, "Thank you, god, for bringing Libby home to me. I promise to take care of her and love her for all eternity. She will always be safe with me."

EPILOGUE

One Year Later
Thanksgiving 1948
Libby

Cuddling up against Jaclyn's bare back as the early morning light streams through our bedroom, I whisper, "Happy second Thanksgiving, beautiful."

Jaclyn wiggles back against my nude body. "Happy Thanksgiving to you, my lovely woman."

Turning toward me, I catch a glimpse of her tempting curves as well as her full bosoms that I've feasted on for the past year. "Damn, you still render me as helpless as an eighteen-year-old, Jaclyn Clarkson."

Laughing loudly, she shouts, "Libby Jordan, you were never a helpless eighteen-year-old!" She continues to laugh at me.

Spanking her, I say, "Well, you're right about that." Poppy jumps up on the bed and gets between us. "Did you hear your

SAILING MRS. CLARKSON

Mama, Poppy? I think she is insinuating that I was a temptress when I was quite young."

Jaclyn rises and puts her blue silk robe over her nude body. She watches me as I gaze at her. "You're breathtaking, Jaclyn."

"If you're trying to get me back in that bed, it won't work. Your family is coming at two o'clock for Thanksgiving dinner, and we have a million things to do."

Crawling nude on my hands and knees toward her slowly, I reach her and ask, "How about if I spank you? Would you crawl back in then?"

Running her fingers through my hair, she gazes down at me and whispers, "You are still that same young temptress. Damn you, Libby."

I purr at her and watch her hunger for me increase. She grabs her Big Ben clock from the side table and winds it without taking her eyes off me. She briefly looks down and sets the timer. She places the clock back on the table, looks at me, and says sternly, "We have one hour!"

Scooping her sideways, I pull her onto the bed with me as she laughs with escalating excitement. I crawl on top of her, peering down at her, and laugh. "Thank you, beautiful. I just wanted to love on you a little while longer."

Touching my lips, she gazes at me. "Libby, I can never say no to you. When you snuggled up against me moments ago, I knew we weren't getting up yet."

Glancing at the clock, I say, "We now have fifty-seven minutes." Then I spank her. Jaclyn laughs excitedly and says, "Come here, Libby Jordan, it's about time that I spank you." With that, Jaclyn aggressively rolls me sideways and spanks my ass.

"Damn, Jaclyn, you're right; those are delightfully wicked," I say as she spanks me again and laughs her delicious sweet laugh.

121

As I prepare the outside table for the family, Jaclyn finishes her cooking inside. I watch her walk out through the French doors of our coastal home. "Libby, this looks incredible. You've decorated beautifully, baby." Poppy trots out with her to join me.

"How many of us will there be, Libby?"

"I've counted fifteen, including us." I draw her to me and say, "Thank you for having my family over for Thanksgiving, Jaclyn.

"Libby, you didn't just say that to me. They're my family too now."

With a huge grin, I nod and say, "Yes, they are. And they love you so much."

"I love them, Libby. They're part of you; how could I not love them?"

"Can you believe Dad?"

"Yes, I can, Libby. When they rebuilt this home for me a couple of years ago, he and I had many conversations over coffee. Your Dad and I think alike in many ways. I like your Dad, baby."

"That makes me happy."

Jaclyn starts sweeping the stone patio, then pauses and looks at me. "I doubt your Dad would have approved of us back then, and who could blame him? Do you think he knows we were lovers back then, Libby?"

I shrug my shoulders and say, "I don't know and will never tell him."

"Well, of course not, baby. That would serve no purpose, but I think somehow he knows Libby, and I'm glad. I wouldn't like the idea of him being displeased with me about that. I don't know why; maybe it's just a matter of respect."

"Jaclyn, we talk about our time back then a lot. Why is that?"

"Libby, It's important. It's our origin story, baby. It's where our love story began," she says as she pushes my hair back with her fingers.

"Yes, it is. That's beautiful, Jaclyn," I say, then kiss her lips gently. "Well, I better get back to my decorating. I'll go inside and check on my Turkey in about thirty minutes. Will you find the Macy's Parade for me on the radio?"

Jaclyn walks up the steps and grabs the handle of the French door. She glances back at me and says, "Yes, I will, baby. But you owe me a dance later tonight."

"I love the sound of that; I'll hold you to it." Jaclyn winks at me, grins, and returns to the kitchen. I shake my head and smile, knowing how happy this woman makes me.

Jaclyn and I sit outside on the back patio at dusk, enjoying a bottle of wine. "Jaclyn, having Thanksgiving out here was wonderful. It was a joyful day, as if everyone has finally healed from Mama's death. I think you deserve much of the credit."

Jaclyn gazes at me for a moment, sips her wine, and asks, "Why would you say that, Libby?"

"Maybe it's because the boys and Dad rebuilt this house. They brought your home to life. A beautiful home you now share with me."

Jaclyn smiles. "Libby, that's very kind, baby."

"I believe they are very happy knowing you take such good care of me. They can see how much we love each other. Maybe our love story is theirs, too."

"Libby, I'm sure there's a lot of truth in what you just said; that's beautiful." Jaclyn stands, kisses me, and says, "I'll be right back." I nod and watch her walk back inside through the French Doors.

After a moment, a soothing and romantic melody drifts through the open French doors, mingling with the cool night air. I smile at Jaclyn, as she walks gracefully toward me, and I stand to meet her. She walks into my arms, pulls me close, and whispers, "Happy second Thanksgiving, my beautiful Libby."

"Awww, Jaclyn, you remembered our dance. I love this song by Sinatra." We move our bodies with the smooth music, finding an intimate rhythm. "You feel incredible in my arms, Jaclyn. We started this tradition last year, so you'll always owe me a dance on Thanksgiving."

Jaclyn looks at me as we continue dancing, and says, "We don't have to wait a whole year, baby. I'll dance with you every night if you want me."

I lean my head against hers and say, "Oh, I definitely want you."

She whispers, "I love you, Libby."

"I love you, Jaclyn. I've never stopped."

THANK YOU

Thank you for reading Sailing Mrs. Clarkson. I hope you enjoyed it.

I'd love it if you could take a minute to leave a review on Amazon and let me know what you thought.

Thanks,
Aven

ALSO BY AVEN BLAIR

Claire's Young Flame

Julian's Lady Luck

Evan's Entanglement

My Sapphires only Dance for Her

Driving Miss Kennedy

Escorting Miss Mercer

ABOUT THE AUTHOR

Aven is a passionate Sapphic romance author living in a charming Southern U.S. town with her wife and their two mischievous Chihuahuas. She crafts compelling narratives about strong Southern women navigating love and life, often set in historical Southern America. Her stories feature steamy age-gap romances, rich with warmth, humor, and depth, captivating readers with unforgettable tales of unwavering dedication.